THE ROCKBED FEUD

A CARSTEN MCNEIL
WESTERN ADVENTURE
BOOK 3

Russell J. Atwater

Contents

Chapter 1
An Open and Shut Case

Phoenix, Arizona, 1892

"All rise for Judge Arma Stanley!" the bailiff called.

Carsten and his deputy, Jack Gibson, sat at the prosecutor's table. They stood up. The defendant, Stan Whitmore, remained seated. He slouched cross-legged and rested his elbows on the back of his chair. He looked at Carsten with an arrogant smirk.

"This is an open-and-shut case," the prosecutor whispered to him. "Why is he looking so confident?"

The judge glowered at the defendant.

"Somethin' ain't right," Carsten replied. "Check the doors, Jack."

A gunshot rang out from the back of the courtroom. Carsten spun around, reaching for his Remington. Those in the gallery pressed against the wall or ran toward the door. Others cowered behind the seats.

A masked man approached the bench with his arm wrapped around a small bespectacled man's neck. He held a revolver in his other hand. "Nobody move!" the man called out. "Let Whitmore go, or else this dude gets it!"

A silence filled the room, broken only by the frightened whimpering of the gunman's hostage.

"You heard him," Whitmore said. He lifted his cuffed hands toward the bailiff. "So how 'bout you do somethin' 'bout these?"

Carsten saw the bailiff glance toward him and then toward the judge.

"Uncuff him!" the gunman snapped. "I ain't foolin' around!"

Carsten heard the fearful tone in the man's voice. "You're makin' a mistake there, friend," he said. "You'd best think 'bout what you're 'bout to do."

"Who are you?" the gunman yelled as he faced Carsten.

"I'm US Marshal Carsten McNeil." He walked out from behind the prosecutor's table with his hands raised. "You may have heard of me. They call me Quaker McNeil because I like to give folks a chance to back down."

"Then you'd best practice what you preach and back off," the gunman replied. "Stan Whitmore is walkin' outta this court a free man."

"We can talk about that," Carsten said. "But we don't need an audience. There ain't no call for nobody else to get hurt."

"Agreed," Judge Stanley's commanding voice interjected. "Bailiff, clear the court." He banged his gavel.

Carsten heard a rush of footsteps as the jurors and gallery audience made their way to the doors. Jack took a position by the door and ushered people out. Carsten positioned himself behind the dispersing crowd. He kept his view fixed on the gunman and his hostage. The footsteps died down as the courtroom cleared.

Carsten moved to the jury box, peering over to see if any of the jurors were hiding. From his position, he saw a solid wall behind the gunman. "Things are little quieter now," he said to the gunman, "so we can talk."

"What about?" the gunman said, raising an eyebrow.

Carsten noticed the man's gun shaking in his hand. "Your situation." Carsten stared him down. "Unless you give up, there's only one way to go, and that's the bone orchard. Even if you shoot your hostage, you'll be dead before you hit the floor. You weren't expectin' resistance, were you?"

"Just let Stan Whitmore go," the gunman said. "I don't want to hurt nobody. I just want Stan Whitmore to be released. You know the judge will make him swing."

"Please, mister," the hostage stammered. "Just give him what he wants."

"Stan Whitmore shot and killed Will Lanning," Carsten continued. "He was unarmed, too. Just walked into the store that was being robbed and took a bullet for bein' in the wrong place at the wrong time. You want a man like that walkin' free? Why?"

"Because he's my older brother..." the gunman said, just as the courtroom doors slammed. He spun his hostage toward the door.

Carsten drew his Remington and fired. The hostage screamed as gun smoke filled the room.

"Ike!" Stan cried out.

Through the haze, Carsten saw the gunman lying on the floor and Stan kneel over the body. The hostage fled the courtroom.

Carsten approached the dead masked man, keeping his gun trained on Whitmore. He kicked Ike's gun out of reach as he viewed the body. Holding his hat to his chest, he saw the hole in the blood-drenched mask. Jack stood by the door as he nodded to him.

"Enough," Whitmore said as tears welled in his eyes. "I surrender and I'll be right behind him. I gotta pay for what I did. Just make sure we're buried right."

The courtroom doors swung open as two more deputies barged in, brandishing shotguns.

"Lower your weapons!" Carsten said as he holstered his gun. 'The dust's settlin'. Are you okay, your honor?"

Judge Stanley stood up. "I'm unharmed," he said. "Good job, Marshal."

"Someone get that fella out of here," Carsten said.

The two deputies slung their guns over their shoulders and dragged the body out of the courtroom. Carsten watched quietly as the people returned.

"The marshal was great!" the former hostage said. "He drew and fired before the gunman could hurt me. That man's a hero." Applause met his remarks. The hostage approached Carsten and shook his hand. "I owe you my life," he said. "And I can't thank you enough."

"I wasn't gonna let no bystanders get hurt," Carsten replied. "It was Deputy Gibson's quick thinkin' that gave me my openin', slammin' the courtroom doors like that."

Jack smiled and nodded in response.

The sound of the gavel interrupted the conversation. "Order in the court!" Judge Stanley called out. "We'll now hear the case of the Arizona Territory versus Stan Whitmore."

The furor died down, and Carsten returned to his seat at the prosecutor's table.

"Stan Whitmore," the judge continued, "you stand here charged with the murder of Will Lanning. How do you plead?"

"Guilty." Whitmore buried his head in his hands.

"Very well," the judge said. "I sentence you to be taken from this place and hanged by the neck until dead. May God have mercy on your soul."

He banged his gavel. Jack escorted the weeping convict out of the courtroom.

***

Carsten felt the late afternoon sun bear down as he left the courthouse. His wife, Fleur, loitered at the foot of the steps, along with a well-dressed man with a notebook and pencil.

"You're safe!" Fleur ran up the steps and embraced him. "When I heard about the shooting, I was so worried!"

"Did you doubt it?" Carsten grinned.

"Marshal McNeil?" The man tapped him on the shoulder.

Carsten rolled his eyes. Fleur smirked.

"I'm Orville Gilbert from the *Daily Phoenx Herald*," the man said. "Do you have a comment on what happened at the courthouse today?"

"Yes." Carsten replied, "Ike Whitmore tried to secure his brother's release by makin' threats. He acted alone and was killed in his attempt. They hurt nobody else." He paused while Orville noted down his statement.

"What about Stan Whitmore?" he asked.

"He's due to hang in the morning for the murder of Will Lanning," Carsten replied. "Hopefully, Mr. Lanning's kin will see justice. Now, if'n you'll excuse me, I'd like to get home with my wife."

"No further questions." The reporter pocketed his notebook and tipped his hat. "You have a good day now."

"Marshal McNeil!" The man who had been taken hostage walked toward the couple with two bottles in his hands. "I'm glad I caught you. I went by your office, and they said you were still at the courthouse."

"What's on your mind?" Carsten said.

"I wanted to give you this Californian red wine as a token of my appreciation." He handed him the bottles. "For saving my life."

"Much obliged." Carsten examined them.

"That might go with those steaks I bought for tonight," Fleur said.

"Sounds real fine." Carsten tipped his hat.

"It's the least I can do," the man replied. "Anyway, I'd better be heading home."

Chapter 2
Homesick

Carsten walked down Mojave Street his arm around Fleur. He tipped his hat to passersby. Riders and the occasional wagon kicked up trail dust, which stuck to his sweat-stained clothes. He nodded to them as he passed. The trees that lined the road and surrounded the courthouse offered little respite from the sun.

"Why do you never want to talk to reporters?" Fleur asked. "Surely you did a good deed today?"

"I don't know," Carsten replied. "I guess I ain't keen on the fanfare because I shot a man who didn't want to see his brother swing. That ain't the kinda thing that's worth celebratin'."

"Surely people want to celebrate the lives you saved?" Fleur said. "They like reading about heroes."

"I guess." Carsten smiled. "I just don't like killin'. My pa retired after he tried to take a life. But I had to take lives 'fore I became a lawman. And I've seen plenty of wannabe gunfighters who read too many dime novels and wanted to be the next Wild Bill Hickok. It never ended well. I guess I don't like the notion of bein' painted a hero and then bein' responsible for that."

"I suppose this is what I miss out on at home," Fleur said.

"I'm sorry, darlin'." Carsten looked at her, "I know you wanted to be a deputy. But the judge didn't see it that way. You're more than welcome to join me as a freelancer, though, like Ramona Vasquez."

"I thought about that," Fleur said. "But I wouldn't get along with her. She's too surly."

They turned a corner on Madison Street and reached a white clapboard bungalow. Carsten removed his boots and held the door open for his wife. She stepped into the kitchen of their two-room house.

***

The smell of cooked meat filled the kitchen. Carsten pressed the steaks against the griddle over the stove. Fleur carried a bowl of potatoes over to the table, where two glasses of wine sat and breathed.

"Just like on the trail." Carsten moved the steaks from the griddle to a pair of plates with corn cobs on them. He took the plates and brought them to the table.

"Looks good." Fleur scooped a helping of potatoes onto the two plates.

Carsten sat down. He bowed his head and clasped his hands.

"Come, Lord Jesus, be our guest," the couple said in unison, "and bless what you have bestowed. Amen."

He picked up his cutlery and cut into his steak, watching the juices ooze out. He bit into the chunk and followed it with a sip of wine. "Rare," he said with a smile. "Just how I like it. And you were right 'bout this wine pairin' with it. Delicious."

Fleur nodded. They clinked glasses and tucked in.

"So how was your day?" he asked.

Fleur ate her dinner in silence.

"Everythin' fine with you?" His brow raised.

She nodded.

"Somethin' on your mind?" Carsten asked. "You just seem real quiet is all."

"I guess I just miss my friends back in Prescott and Cripple Gorge," she replied.

"Me too." Carsten looked into his wine. "Given the choice, I would have stayed in Prescott if this posting allowed me to do so. But since the federal court moved to Phoenix, I had to as well. At least we didn't miss Attie's wedding. Been a while since we had a decent shindig."

"Carsten…" she said, "you promised this posting would be temporary. I hardly know anyone in this town. The deputies' wives seem nice enough, but I feel out of place. Maybe I'm not used to being a housewife."

"I get that," he replied. "It's been hard on both of us with the move. And I ain't always around when I'm on the trail of this territory's most wanted. That business with the dirty sheriff didn't help much. A couple of folks are still sore at that. You earned your spurs long ago, but I guess when the railroads came and towns started gettin' civilized, a status quo from back east came out west."

"Then what do we do?"

"I reckon we bear it for a little while longer." Carsten took another sip of wine. "The judge will probably have another list of warrants for me to serve. I'm comin' to the end of my term soon, and Gibson's a fella I can tie to. I might recommend him to replace me. When all is done, I reckon I can go back to ranchin'. I'm still a part owner of Pa's spread. We'll be back in Prescott soon enough. I promise." He reached across the table and clasped Fleur's hand.

She returned it.

"And maybe we can work on introducing some little McNeils too," he added with a smile.

Chapter 3
An Unpleasant Dispute

Hank Patterson walked his horse behind his flock, down the trail that ran through Pleasant Valley. His son Aaron, a red-haired boy of fifteen years, rode alongside the flank to keep the flock on the trail. He pulled his hat low to avoid the glare of the morning sun. A chorus of bleats from his sheep filled the air.

Three riders appeared on the trail. Their bandanas and chaps gave them away as cattle hands. They rode toward the flock. Hank and his son halted.

"What do you reckon, Pa?" Aaron brought his horse parallel to Hank's.

"I don't know, son." Hank's grip on his reins tightened. "Just keep your head and let me do the talkin'."

Two of the riders rode around the front of Hank's flock. Unable to move forward, the sheep milled about.

The third rider rode past them toward Hank and Aaron. "Howdy." He tipped his hat to Hank. "Where are you takin' the woolies there?"

"To the pasture meadow, if that's any of your business," Hank replied.

"It is." The rider scratched the back of his head. "This here trail sits on Mr. Boon's land. And the good grazin' is gettin' kinda scarce for his beeves."

"I thought the pasture meadow's open to anybody," Hank replied. "And you know that meadow's better suited to sheep than cattle."

"There ain't nothin' wrong with y'all bringin' the woolies to pasture," the rider said, "but they tramplin' a lot of the grass that's for our cattle. We're gonna need some kind of recompense for that."

"But I've used this trail countless times," Hank said. "I've never had to pay no toll before."

"I can't help that." The rider held out his hand. "It's gonna cost you five dollars to drive the woolies through here."

"Five dollars?" Aaron piped up. "That's borderin' on daylight robbery!"

"Quiet, boy," Hank said in a low tone. "Don't give them a reason to shoot us."

"You'd best listen to your pa, son." The rider rested his hand on his holster. "If you ain't payin' the toll, you're trespassin'."

A bead of sweat ran down Hank's forehead. He exchanged glances with his son and the riders. The two men in front of the flock had their hands resting on holsters as well.

"Pa…" Aaron said.

"Fine." Hank reached into his pocket for a handful of coins. He counted out five silver dollars and handed them to the leader of the group.

The man smirked as he listening to the clinking of the coins. "Much obliged." He tipped his hat. "You have a good day now. And don't spend too long roundin' them up. We'll shoot any stragglers."

"I want to speak to Mr. Boon about this," Hank said.

"He's busy." The rider turned his horse around and rode away with his companions.

***

As they reached the pasture, Hank started into the distance.

"What the hell is Mr. Boon doin'?" Aaron said. "It ain't right we gotta pay no damn toll to take our sheep anyplace."

"Watch your cussin', boy." Hank glared at him. "There ain't no sense in gettin' killed over a few sheep."

"But everyone knows Mr. Boon hates sheep farmers." Aaron whined. "He'll bleed us dry so he can buy our land for his herds to graze on."

Hank fell silent. He pondered his son's words.

"We gotta do somethin', or that bastard is gonna walk all over us for the rest of our days." Aaron said.

"Language!" Hank snapped, and let out a sigh. "You're right. But we can't just fight him ourselves. We gotta speak to the sheriff in Rockbed. I'll raise it with him."

***

Hank trotted down the trail to Rockbed. A handful of people walked down the main street, looking for shade as the afternoon approached.

"You wait here." He dismounted and hitched his horse outside the sheriff's office.

"But, Pa..." Aaron said.

"No buts, boy," Hank said. "This is grown-up talk. You watch the horses and find some shade. I won't be long."

The interior of the sheriff's office smelled of must. Hank twitched as he stepped inside. Sheriff Willie Snow, a rotund man with a full beard, sat behind his desk with his feet up and his hat pulled down over his eyes. Hank cleared his throat.

The sheriff grunted and lifted his hat. "Mr. Patterson," he said.

"Howdy, Sheriff," Hank replied. "I gotta report somethin' that happened this mornin'."

"Go ahead." Snow put his feet down.

"I was takin' my flock out to pasture with Aaron." Hank sat down in the chair in front of Snow's desk. "We got met by some boys from Milt Boon's spread. They said we was trespassin' and demanded we pay a toll."

"And?" Snow replied with a shrug.

"Well, I've been that trail regular for some time," Hank said. "I never had to pay no toll."

"I know the trail you mean," Snow replied. "Sorry to say it, but that land belongs to Mr. Boon. There ain't nothin' illegal about a fella gettin' recompense for damages to grazing land."

"But he demanded five bucks." Hank massaged his temples. "I don't have that much money to spare if I have to pay that every time."

"I can't do nothin' bout that." Snow eased out of his chair. He moved to a stove and poured himself a cup of coffee.

"Can't or won't?" Patterson said.

Snow stopped pouring. He turned to Hank with a scowl. "No laws have been broken," he said. "I ain't gonna pick no fights with Mr. Boon. Unless you got evidence he's doin' somethin' illegal, I can't do anythin' 'bout it. And if'n you're gonna make baseless claims 'bout him, he could be gettin' a judge to charge you with libel."

Hank stepped outside onto the decking in front of the sheriff's office. He slammed the door behind him.

Aaron emerged from his shaded spot behind the barbershop next to the sheriff's office. "How'd it go?" he asked.

"You didn't hear the shoutin'?" Hank unhitched the horses. "The sheriff ain't gonna do a thing since demandin' a toll on your own land ain't illegal."

"So what do we do?" Aaron mounted his horse.

"We gotta put up with it," Hank said. "At least, until I can arrange somethin' with Milt."

"And when will that be?" Aaron replied. "He'll bleed us dry, dammit."

"I told you to watch your cussin'." Hank raised an index finger to his son. "One more profanity or blasphemy, and you'll be goin' without supper tonight. Understood?"

"Yes, sir." Aaron bowed his head.

"Come on." Hank patted him on the shoulder. "Let's go home. I'll figure somethin' out. Sooner or later, somebody's gonna get even with Milt. You can count on that."

Chapter 4
New Warrants

The smell of freshly brewed coffee greeted Carsten. Gibson stood by the stove as three other deputies loitered around the office. Nastas, a Navajo deputy, sat in the corner cleaning a rifle while ignoring the idle chatter. He stood up as Carsten entered. Moses Brennan, a burly deputy with a bushy mustache, leaned against the wall by the door with his arms folded. Pete Wilkins, a one-armed deputy with three revolvers on his gun belt, sat in one of the two chairs in front of Carsten's desk with his feet resting on the other.

"Mornin', boys," Carsten said. The idle chatter ceased.

"I saved some coffee for you, Marshal McNeil." Gibson poured a spare cup and handed it to him.

"Much obliged." Carsten moved his stack of papers to under his other arm to take the cup.

"How's Mrs. McNeil holdin' up, Marshal?" Wilkins asked. "Mabel's sayin' she hasn't been around much lately."

"She's fine." Carsten sat down in the chair behind the desk. "Reckon she's gettin' homesick for Prescott. But family's gonna have to wait." He laid down the papers across the desk.

"More kindling for the fire?" Wilkins peered over at the papers.

"If you mean a new set of warrants." Carsten sipped his coffee. "Collected them from Judge Stanley this mornin'."

"Who we goin' after?" Moses asked.

"We'll start with Bowman Ratcliff." Carsten flipped through the warrants and produced the handbill. "Turns out he and his boys held up that mail flyer on its way to Phoenix yesterday. Reckon they're goin' to ground in the mountains. Nastas, you reckon you can track them?"

Nastas nodded.

"Then we'd best make a move," Carsten said. "Finish your coffee and be ready to head out."

"Who else is on the list?" Gibson asked.

"Let me check." Carsten flicked through the warrants. "Blaine Weber, wanted for stealin' horses in Globe, last seen in Florence. Alvin McIntyre and Mitchel Winn, wanted in connection with a stagecoach robbery in Bisbee, believed to have gone to ground somewhere in Tucson. And Todd Moony, wanted for murder. Last seen in Globe. Reckon it's gonna be a busy few weeks, so you'd best tell your wives you're gonna be gone for a while. We'll use today to get any supplies we need, but we'll ride out in the morning. There's a stage headin' out tomorrow that might draw them out. Especially since they're carryin' silver."

***

The following morning, Carsten cinched his saddle to Dan, his chestnut gelding. He tipped his hat to the livery owner and led the horse out. Fleur stood by the door and watched him.

"This is one part of this job I hate." Carsten said. "Unless, of course, you want to ride with me. I could always use an extra gun."

Fleur said nothing.

"Don't worry, darlin'." Carsten threw his arms around her. "I ain't gonna be gone long. Just a few days."

"Be careful." Fleur returned the embrace.

"I'll be back real soon," he said with a smile. The sound of approaching hooves and the trundle of wheels made his ears perk.

A stagecoach pulled to a halt near the livery's corral, where Nastas waited on his own horse. Moses sat beside the driver, carrying a shotgun.

"We're all set, Marshal." Gibson followed behind on his own horse.

"That's my cue." Carsten picked up the Winchester propped against the livery wall and stowed it in his saddle ring. "I'll see you soon. Unless you want to ride in the stagecoach."

"You know what?" she replied. "I think I might."

Carsten walked her over to the stagecoach and opened the door. Wilkins sat inside. He tipped his hat to her.

"You know what you gotta do?" Carsten asked.

"Keep to the stage and keep my shootin' irons within my reach," Wilkins replied. "Don't you worry, Marshal. This ain't the first gunfight I've been in since losin' the arm. I got my system in place. And I'll watch your wife."

"Do I get a gun too?" Fleur asked.

"Here." Carsten handed her his Remington. He reached into his pocket and produced two extra cylinders. She nodded and took them.

"You're armin' a civilian?" Wilkins raised a brow. "I know she's your wife and all, but ain't you takin' a big a risk?"

"Not as big a risk as some we both took in the past." Carsten stared Wilkins down. "She wanted to ride with us, and she's welcome to."

"Of course, Marshal," Wilkins said. "I didn't mean to give no offense. But where are you gonna be?"

"I'll be followin' you with Gibson and Nastas," Carsten said. "We'll keep outta sight as best we can. If'n they chase the stage, we'll be right behind them. If'n they stop the stage, we can cut off their escape."

Carsten mounted his horse and walked out of the corral. He blew a kiss to Fleur, who nodded in response. The stagecoach driver flicked the reins. Carsten watched the stage roll out of town.

***

By midday, Carsten felt the sweat soak his shirt. He stared toward the Estrella Mountains. The stagecoach rolled ahead of them.

"Everythin' all right, Marshal?" Gibson brought his mount parallel to Carsten and Dan.

"Just hopin' this works," Carsten replied.

"You worried 'bout your wife?" Gibson asked.

"A little," Carsten said. "She's been in gunfights before, and she's one of the bravest people I ever met."

"She's been in gunfights?" Gibson's eyes widened.

"Before I was a lawman, some rip who wanted my family's land kidnapped my sister," Carsten said. "Me and my brother assembled a posse to get her back, and Fleur joined us. Then there was that business with the killin' of Marshal Cooper. She was caught in the middle of that, just as I was. If the judge hadn't blocked it, I would have made her a deputy. You've worked with Ramona Vasquez, haven't you?"

"I've heard of her, but I haven't worked with her," Gibson replied.

Ahead, the stagecoach turned at a fork in the trail, heading onto a road through the mountains.

"Better get ready." Carsten eased the Winchester out of his saddle ring. He led his deputies into a canyon, as he kept Dan moving at a trot.

The wagon turned a bend and disappeared from view. He gestured for his deputies to slow to a walk. The rumble of the stagecoach resounded further up the trail. It stopped, drowned out by the whinnying of the team.

"They've stopped," Carsten said under his breath. He turned the corner. A pile of rocks obstructed the trail.

Six armed men surrounded the wagon. The driver had let go of the reins, and he and Moses had their hands in the air.

"Throw down that scattergun," one man said with a commanding voice that echoed through the canyon.

Carsten nodded to Nastas, who dismounted and moved up to a cluster of rocks with his rifle. Carsten and Gibson walked their horses toward the stagecoach.

"US Marshals!" Carsten shouted. "Drop your weapons and throw up your hands! You're under arrest!"

Two of the bandits behind the stagecoach spun around. They raised their guns. Carsten cocked his rifle.

The bandit with the commanding voice, stepped forward. The clink of his spurs broke the silence. "Well, well, well." He rested his hands on his hips. "If ain't Marshal Carsten 'Quaker' McNeil. You come to save the day?"

"You must be Bowman Ratcliff." Carsten kept his rifle trained on him. "Robbed the mail carrier while they tied me up with the incident at the courthouse."

"What can I say?" Ratcliff removed his mask to show his cheeky grin. "The opportunity was there, so I took it. You have some mighty gumption comin' out here with one other man. Or is the shotgun messenger one of yours too?"

The sounds of revolvers cocked from inside the stage. Wilkins aimed one of his revolvers out the stagecoach window.

"So that's four of you?" Ratcliff sneered. "Or three and a half?"

The other bandits laughed. Fleur aimed Carsten's Remington out the opposite window.

"Five," she said.

"You'd better put the gun down, ma'am," Ratcliff said. "You're liable to get hurt if lead starts flyin'."

"Driver, give him the strongbox." Carsten looked back at Ratcliff. "That's what you came for, right?"

The strongbox hit the ground next to Moses's discarded shotgun.

"Open it up!" Ratcliff barked to one of his men.

Another robber kneeled down and opened the strongbox. He pulled out a small sack that made a metallic rattling sound. Two others crowded around the sack and reached inside. They scooped out the contents.

"This ain't silver," one said. "It's steel washers. It's a trick!" The man leveled his revolver at Carsten. A shot rang out from behind Carsten, and the man fell back.

"Tarnation!" Ratcliff reached for his revolver.

Carsten fired his Winchester. The bullet struck Ratcliff's arm. The gun flew out of his hand and he screamed. Shots echoed from within the wagon. The bandits returned fire and fled to the rocks. Carsten chambered the next round and fired again. Another bandit dropped to the floor. Ratcliff knelt down and scrambled for his lost gun. Carsten dismounted and aimed at Ratcliff. The robber froze.

"Cease fire!" Carsten shouted.

The smoke cleared. The three remaining bandits threw away their guns and raised their hands. Carsten gestured for Ratcliff to stand and herded him to his three companions. The doors of the stagecoach swung open. Wilkins and Fleur stepped out, their pistols trained on the gang.

"Everyone okay?" Carsten asked.

"I'm fine," Gibson replied.

"Me too." Fleur said.

"Fine as cream gravy," Wilkins said. "Didn't even need my second gun."

"All good," Moses replied. He remained in his seat atop the stagecoach with his revolver drawn.

"Nice work," Carsten said. "Gibson, make sure they're cuffed. Wilkins, Fleur, and Brennan keep them covered. We'll take them back in the stagecoach."

Gibson dismounted and stowed his rifle. He handed his gun to Carsten and approached the men. After Ratcliff and his men were handcuffed and restrained, Wilkins held open the stagecoach door. Carsten gestured for them to enter.

"What about the other two?" Gibson asked. He pointed at the bodies.

"We'll take the gang's horses," Carsten replied. "Brennan, you get the bodies loaded up onto one of them. We'll see they're identified and given a decent burial. Gibson, help Wilkins onto the rumble seat. Fleur, you take one of the spare horses. And thanks for the help, darlin'."

"Anytime," she replied. "Nice to be workin' with you again."

Chapter 5
A Generous Offer

Hank Patterson raised his axe and then swung it down, splitting the log in two. He picked up a half and chopped it. The morning sun shone on the yard. His house provided little shade near the wood storage. He placed another log onto the block and raised the axe. The blade embedded in the log causing Hank to lift the axe and the log. Sweat poured down his face. He slammed the log against the block. The blade cut through the log and embedded in the block.

"Pa!" Aaron called.

Hank looked up as two riders appeared on the horizon.

"Are they Frazer's boys?" Aaron said. "What do you reckon they want?"

"I don't know, son." Hank gripped the axe. "Get back inside. I'll handle this." Hank ushered his son into the farmhouse.

His wife, Esther, looked up from the washbasin. "Hank?" she asked. "What's going on?"

"We've got riders comin'." Hank grabbed a shotgun hanging above the mantelpiece. "Both of you, stay inside. Aaron, mind your ma. Understood?"

"Yes, sir," Aaron said with a higher pitch.

Hank patted him on the shoulder.

The riders entered the yard.

Hank stepped onto his porch with the shotgun. "That's far enough," he said. "Stop right there and state your business."

The two riders yanked their reins. Their horses halted. Hank looked them over. He recognized one rider as one of Milt's trail hands from when he'd been accosted on the way to the pasture. The second man had three scars on one side of his face, along with a perpetual scowl. His trail clothes looked new. Hank swallowed. He recognized the man as Norman Reid, Milt Boon's foreman.

"There's no need for that." Reid pointed at the shotgun and glared at Hank.

Hank gave a curt nod. He propped the gun against the wall.

"Mr. Boon would like to talk to you," Reid said.

"Right now?" Hank asked.

"Right now," Reid said.

"Aaron!" Hank called. His son peered through the door. "Saddle the horses. I'm gonna meet with Mr. Boon."

"Yes, sir." Aaron ran to the barn.

Esther stepped out onto the porch. She noticed Hank's pale complexion. "Would you gentlemen like some coffee before you leave?" she asked.

"No, thank you, ma'am," Reid said in a softer tone. "We ain't plannin' on hangin' around here too long. Mr. Boon's a very busy man, and it won't be a good idea to keep him waitin'."

Hank fidgeted. Reid aimed a sharp glance at him. He ran to the barn, where Aaron emerged, leading a horse. "Thanks, boy," he said as he mounted. "If I ain't back by sundown, get the sheriff."

Aaron nodded.

Hank walked his horse over to Reid and the other trail hand. "Shall we head off?"

***

After an hour and a half of riding, the group arrived at the Boon ranch. Hank raised his eyebrows at the compound. Surrounded by an adobe wall, it resembled a fort rather than a ranch. The trail led to a small shack opposite a large wooden gate. A man with a repeater stood outside the shack. He nodded to Reid and moved to pull the gates open. He beckoned for Hank to enter.

Hank rode through the gates into a large outer courtyard. He looked around. Ahead lay a two-story plantation house. A barn sat close to the gate. Other adobe structures of varying sizes scattered the compound. Chickens and pigs wandered around. A group of men played horseshoes in front of the barn. More men loitered around the other buildings. Some carried rifles.

Reid led Hank to a hitching post by the house. Hank dismounted. He exchanged a stare with one rough-looking man loitering by the hitching post, who spun the cylinder of a revolver. Hank heard his own heart beating as he heard the dull whir of the cylinder. The man spat a wad of tobacco juice near Hank's feet.

Hank followed Reid to the porch, where a lean man in a white suit sat at a small table, sipping a cup of coffee. On the table was a tray with an ornate metal coffee pot and a china cup and saucer, a small jug of cream and a bowl of sugar. A silver-headed walking stick rested by his chair.

"Hank Patterson, boss," Reid said.

"Morning, Mr. Patterson." The man in white spoke with an articulate southern accent. He stood up and extended his hand. "Glad you accepted my invitation."

"I didn't realize that was an invitation," Hank said under his breath. He clenched his teeth as he felt Milt Boon's firm handshake. "I'd like to talk about an incident that happened yesterday."

"I bet you do," Milt replied. "But why don't you sit yourself down and have some coffee?"

Hank looked back at Reid, who leaned against the wall with his arms folded. He sat down and poured the coffee into the cup.

"Things have been difficult lately," Boon said. "Good grazing land is getting hard to find for my cattle, and I'm needing to expand, take on more ranch hands, and buy more feed. But I'm going to need to get some working capital in order to fund that."

"So that's why you're gettin' your men to demand a toll?" Hank added a spoonful of sugar to his coffee. "I thought the pastureland was supposed to be unrestricted. That's what you agreed with Frazer and me. It ain't fit for cattle, so you said you'd offer it for grazin' sheep."

"And I have upheld that bargain." Boon leaned back and clasped his hands. "But you were driving your sheep across my land. I have a right to demand reparations."

"But do they have to charge five dollars?" Hank stirred his coffee and took a drink. "That seems kinda high in terms of prices, especially if it's something I gotta pay each time I pass through. Do you charge Frazer that much?"

"I will charge everyone the tax," Boon replied. "Or at least, everyone who needs to pass through. Mr. Frazer has another pasture that doesn't cross my land. I'm surprised you don't go to him."

"I did." Hank's grip tightened on his cup. "He refused, tellin' me to use the common pasture."

"He's not being very neighborly," Boon said, "But I'd like to offer you a proposition. Frazer's land is suited well to cattle. Perhaps if he was out of the picture, I could graze my herds there. Perhaps if you could help me acquire it?"

"What's in it for me?" Hank shrugged.

"We'll be partners," Boon said. "I can graze my cattle on your land. You can graze your sheep on mine. No tolls."

Hank fidgeted. He finished his coffee and set the cup down.

The sound of shouting echoed from a single-story adobe house on the opposite side of the compound.

"Reid," Boon said in a commanding voice.

Reid nodded and walked over to the house.

"What's happenin'?" Hank peered over. "That the bunkhouse?"

"In a manner of speaking," Boon replied. "Will you excuse me? You can think about my offer until I come back. Make yourself comfortable. This won't take long." He picked up the walking stick and followed Reid.

Hank peered over to see where the two men went.

"The boss told you to stay put," the man by the hitching post said.

Hank looked at the gun in the man's hands. He shrugged and leaned back in his chair. A rock landed by the guard's feet, tapping along the porch. The guard cocked his gun and walked away to investigate.

Hank stepped off the porch. A red-haired woman in a ragged dress waved to him from the corner of the porch. He walked over.

"You're not one of Mr. Boon's men." She spoke in a hushed tone, looking over both shoulders.

"No, I'm not," Hank replied. "The name's Hank Patterson. I run a sheep farm."

"Can you do something for me?" She produced a letter from her dress sleeve. "Take this to my brother in Boston."

"Take what?" Boon returned to the porch with Reid. "Are you disturbing my guest, Miss Filmore?"

She stowed the letter. Reid led her away by the arm.

"What's goin' on here?" Hank asked.

"A couple of my hands got into a fight," Boon said. "Some disagreement over a poker game."

"I didn't mean that," Hank said. "I was wonderin' 'bout the girl."

"Ah, the lovely Miss Amy Filmore," Boon said. "It is a given the world over that when a bunch of cowboys reach the end of a trail drive, they spend their money getting liquored up, and that often leads to violence. So I came up with a solution. Would you like to see?"

"I think I oughta be gettin' back." Hank stroked his beard.

"You don't have to stay." Boon placed a hand on Hank's shoulder. "But you might as well take a look. You might appreciate a little southern hospitality this far west."

Hank followed Boon to the adobe house. Ahead of them, Reid walked with Amy.

The interior of the structure carried a strong smell of spilled booze and cigar smoke. A small bar took up the corner of the room, with bottles of whiskey and tequila. One man in a tobacco-stained bowler hat polished a glass. Four men sat around a table, playing poker. Four Mexican women in threadbare dresses loitered around the area. They stretched and gave other suggestive poses, but in a half-hearted manner. Reid led Amy down the hallway.

"Mr. Patterson, welcome to Boon's Cantina," Boon said with a proud smile. "Many times I've had to square up issues in the town after my men caused trouble. So why not offer an exclusive watering hole for my employees? Care for a whiskey?"

"No, thanks." Hank raised his hand.

"With cards, drinks, and a few women, there's no need for my men to go into town," Boon continued. "I could deliver all the vices a hardworking trail hand wants to their very doorstep."

"I see," Hank said. "But don't that just bring the trouble away from the towns to your doorstep?"

"There is the occasional fist fight." Boon said. "But they are resolved quickly. Ever since Mr. Reid was taken on as my foreman, the number of serious incidents has declined."

"I ain't surprised," Hank said in a low tone. "Everyone has heard of Mr. Reid. He once killed a man for snorin'. And plenty more for breathin'."

He fell silent as Reid walked back into the room without Amy.

"His reputation precedes him." Boon nodded. "You see, I believe in forgiveness. A lot of men have come to my ranch looking for gainful employment. Many of those men have been involved in illegal activities in the past, and I want to reform them. Of course, not everyone settles down right away, so I hired Mr. Reid to ensure they do. People are less likely to get too wild if they think that will make Mr. Reid angry. I can help these people square things with the laws of God, but not the laws of the territories or states they came from. With this in mind, I've come up with another proposition."

"I'm listenin'…" Hank fidgeted.

"A lot of these men have outstanding warrants." A stern tone replaced Boon's warm and outgoing demeanor. "And I cannot risk them facing the gallows for their troubled pasts. What happens behind these walls stays behind those walls. Is that clear?"

Hank slinked back as Boon stared at him. He nodded.

"I'm so glad you agree." Boon patted him on the shoulder and returned to his warm tone. "In fact, I would like to offer you twenty head of cattle if you agree to this stipulation. How does that sound?"

"Really?" Hank stammered. "If'n I can't get no decent price for sheep at the market, a few longhorns would be a nice thing to fall back on. It's a deal." He shook Boon's hand.

"Shall we drink to this new partnership?" Boon asked. "We don't need to drink here. I have some brandy back at the house."

Chapter 6
The Next Warrant

Passersby stopped to stare at the procession returning to Phoenix. Carsten escorted the stagecoach toward the jail. He tipped his hat toward the onlookers. Fleur rode sidesaddle parallel to him, while Nastas and Gibson led the Ratcliff gang's spare horses. The bodies of two of the gang members were slung over one horse.

Carsten dismounted Dan and secured him to the hitching post as the driver brought the stagecoach to a halt. Carsten grabbed his Winchester. Moses and Wilkins took up a position by the door. Moses aimed his shotgun at the door.

"Gibson, get the cells open," Carsten said. He opened the stagecoach door.

Bowman Ratcliff and his three companions sat inside, their hands cuffed behind their backs.

"All of you, out!" Wilkins cocked his revolver.

Ratcliff stepped outside. He winced as he caught his arm on the door. His companions followed. Carsten ushered the prisoners into the cells and Gibson led each man to an empty cell. He uncuffed their hands and locked the cell doors behind him.

"What shall we do about the bodies, Marshal?" the deputy asked.

"We'll organize burials," Carsten replied. "Get the undertaker. And get a doctor to look at Ratcliff's arm. Once we finish the reports, the drinks are on me."

The deputies cheered. Gibson left the office. Carsten returned his rifle to the cabinet in his office. He sat behind his desk and grabbed a pencil. Fleur stepped inside. He smiled at her.

"Thanks for your help, darlin'," he said. "You did great."

"Makes a change from languishing at home." Fleur stroked his chin.

Judge Stanley appeared in the doorway. "Marshal McNeil."

"I'll see you at home," Carsten whispered to Fleur. He stood up. "What can I do for you, your honor?"

"I'd like to speak to you in private, if you don't mind," he said. "Would you be able to accompany me back to the courthouse?"

"Right away." Carsten stood up. "Wilkins, can you and Moses take care of the reports? I'll look at them when I get back."

"Sure thing, Marshal," Wilkins said.

"May I come too?" Fleur asked. "This might concern me."

Carsten glanced between his wife and the judge.

Stanley gave a nod. "You're welcome to walk with us, Mrs. McNeil," he said. "But the meeting is a private matter between me and your husband."

***

The interior of the judge's chamber smelled of floor polish. The blinds cast the room in shadow, but the open window did little to ease the heat. Carsten removed his hat as he entered. Fleur sat down on a chair in the hallway. She peered inside the chamber until the judge closed the door behind him.

"Sit down, Carsten." Stanley gestured to a chair in front of the desk.

He fidgeted when he heard the judge refer to him by name. "What do you want to talk about, your honor?" Carsten sat down.

"A couple of matters." Stanley sat behind the desk. He clasped his hands. "You have done sterling work in your tenure as a US Marshal. I must congratulate you on how you apprehended the Bowman Ratcliff gang. But I have an issue with you regularly including your wife in your posse."

"Your honor..." Carsten began. The judge scowled at him, so he fell silent.

"Thank you," the judge said. "I've heard plenty of stories about Fleur traveling with you. I've heard you talk about how capable she is, so save it. It wouldn't be right for a serving US Marshal to appoint their own family as deputies. You know about what happened with the Earps?"

"Yes, your honor." Carsten nodded.

"Then you understand the dangers of nepotism. These towns are getting civilized, and I want to demonstrate to newcomers that we have family values like at home. How would it look if your wife got killed while hunting a felon? This is your final warning. If I hear Mrs. McNeil is riding with you again, it will force me to charge you with contempt and may even have you dismissed from the service."

"I understand." Carsten bowed his head.

"I'm glad," Stanley replied. "You're a good lawman, and I hate to lose you. Who's next on your list?"

"Blaine Weber, your honor. Horse thief. I reckon he'll try to resist with charges like that. Last seen in Florence."

"Then you have your next warrant," Stanley said. "That'll be all, Marshal. Go talk to your wife."

Carsten nodded and left the judge's chamber.

Fleur sat on a bench in the hallway and fidgeted. She perked up as Carsten shut the door to the chamber. "What's wrong?"

"Let's walk and talk." Carsten offered a hand and led her downstairs. He spoke in a solemn tone.

Fleur's smile faded.

Gibson waited in the foyer at the bottom of the stairs. "The reports are on your desk, Marshal. The doc has seen Ratcliff too. He'll make it to trial."

"Much obliged, Gibson," Carsten replied. "I'll look at them later. Get three deputies together at dawn tomorrow. We'll be ridin' out to Florence. I'll meet y'all then. For now, I'm headin' home."

"I'll arrange it," Gibson said.

"Here." Carsten reached into his pocket and produced a dollar bill. "You and the rest of the deputies have a couple of whiskeys on me. Celebrate today's arrests."

***

The sun set as Carsten and Fleur huddled around their table. Carsten stared into the dregs of his coffee cup.

"Traditional family values?" Fleur said.

"That's what he called it. I don't like it. Not one bit."

"But we were partners," Fleur said. Tears welled in her eyes. "I didn't marry you to stick to being a housewife."

"And I ain't askin' you to become a housewife." Carsten held her hand. "But the judge ain't happy. He ain't exactly sayin' you gotta be a housewife, neither. He's just sayin' you can't ride with me."

"That's the same thing." Fleur shook her head. "Maybe it's a sign we should go back to Prescott."

"Fleur," Carsten said in a soft tone. "You know how people like to share stories in these parts? How would it look if they dismissed me as a marshal because I deputized you against Judge Stanley's wishes? Almost everybody 'd shun us. Not just here, but in Prescott too."

"What about when you got framed for Marshal Cooper's murder? People talked then. People still do, even after your name got cleared. We can return to your family's ranch. They always understood us."

"I'm sorry." Carsten sighed. "I'd rather finish my term on a high note. There ain't long to go, and we can move back to Prescott once I'm done. I promise that."

Fleur turned away and fled into the bedroom.

Carsten heard her crying. "What the hell am I doing?" he said to himself.

***

Dawn came. Carsten loitered outside his office with Dan while his deputies inspected saddles and weapons. He ignored a conversation between Moses and Wilkins. He looked at the tailor shop across the road from the office. A shop assistant readied two fancy dresses on mannequins in the shop window.

"Everything all right, Marshal?" Gibson asked. "You seem kinda distracted."

"Well, I guess I never thought I'd find myself torn between love and duty like this," Carsten replied.

"Trouble at home?" Gibson patted him on the shoulder.

"Judge wasn't too happy 'bout Fleur ridin' with us," Carsten said. "He's said I can't take her with us no more. So we argued 'bout it last night. I'm wonderin' if I should quit and move back to Prescott where our family's based. But I at least wanna get through this backlog of warrants before I finish my term."

"I'm sorry," Gibson said. "That ain't right. Fleur is one of the bravest women I ever met. It's a shame the judge don't see things that way. Maybe she'll come around, eventually. How long are we gonna be gone for, you reckon?"

"It's a two-day ride to Florence."

"Then maybe that'll be for the best," Gibson replied. "Perhaps you need a couple of days apart to cool down. I often find that with Rowena. We don't always see eye to eye, but after I'm on the trail for a couple of days, we always look forward to bein' back in each other's arms."

"Thanks for the advice." Carsten gave him a weak smile. "Okay, fellas. Time to mount up."

He climbed into the saddle. Moses helped Wilkins mount his own horse. Carsten flicked the reins and spurred Dan on.

***

The sun was setting as the posse reached the outskirts of Florence. Carsten stroked his chin.

"Where do we start lookin', Marshal?" Gibson asked.

"We'll check with the sheriff," Carsten replied. "Then we'll search the saloons and whorehouses. If he's in town, he's likely gonna be eager for a few drinks, a card came, or a girl."

"And if he ain't in town?" Wilkins asked.

"Then we keep followin' his trail," Carsten said. "Florence is a small town, so it won't take long to find him. With any luck, we'll catch him with his pants down. Like that fella in Tombstone."

The other deputies laughed at the reminder.

"You mean Two-Gun Mickey?" Wilkins said.

"The very same." Carsten grinned. "I think everyone learned the origin of that name through that misadventure."

The posse trotted through the main street. Shopkeepers were closing their storefronts and making their way to the saloons. Boisterous singing and yelling emanated from one saloon, which many townspeople gave a wide berth. Carsten hitched his horse outside the sheriff's office. He pushed the door open. Inside, three men sat around a desk, loading revolvers and repeaters.

"Can I help you?" A clean-shaven man with a shotgun looked up.

"I'm US Marshal Carsten McNeil." Carsten pulled back the lapel of his duster coat to reveal his badge. "I'm lookin' for a fella by the name of Blaine Weber, last seen 'round here."

"My name's Grover Moon, Pinal County Sheriff," the man replied. "I ain't familiar with anybody of that name. You got a handbill?"

Carsten produced a folded-up sheet of paper from his pocket. He handed it to the sheriff.

"I ain't seen nobody with that face 'round here." Grover studied the poster. "But I've got a problem with some rips who are drunk in the saloon and threatenin' to shoot up the whole town. Those boys outnumber mine, so I could use some help. Maybe your man's among them."

"We ain't got time for county matters," Wilkins hissed to Carsten, who gestured for silence.

"We'll help you if'n you help us," Carsten replied.

A nod and a hand gesture got all the men to head out. Carsten followed the sheriff and his deputies toward the saloon. The yelling within grew louder, accompanied by the frantic tapping of a piano's keys. A patron tumbled through the batwing doors, landing at Carsten's feet.

"What's goin' on in there, mister?" Carsten asked.

"It's some trail crew." The patron scrambled to his feet. "They're claimin' the saloon for what they call a private shindig. They're liquored up and wavin' guns around."

"Sheriff, take your deputies and head around the back," Carsten said. "Rest of you with me. Don't go shootin' unless they shoot first." Carsten stepped through the batwing doors.

A layer of spilled whiskey and tobacco juices covered the floor, dotted by empty bottles. A group of ten ranch hands occupied the saloon. One man tapped away a butchered tune on the piano. Another man swung on the chandelier. He fell through a table in the center of the room. An uproar of laughter followed.

"Hey, this a private shindig." One man lumbered over to Carsten. "You'd best skedaddle or I'll get mad." He patted the revolver in his waistband.

Carsten snatched the gun and swung it into the man's face.

"Dang it!" the drunkard screamed and reeled back.

The piano music halted. The other trail hands stared.

"We're here to disarm you," Carsten said. "Throw up your hands."

Sheriff Moon and his deputies entered through the back door. They punctuated the silence by cocking their rifles.

"Disarm my caboose." The drunkard unsheathed a Bowie knife.

"Carsten, look out!" Gibson yelled.

"Carsten?" The drunkard stopped at the mention of the name. "Carsten McNeil?" He dropped the knife. A clatter followed as the other men dropped their guns.

"Now that I have your attention," Carsten said, "do any of you gentlemen know someone with the handle of Blaine Weber?"

The trail hands fell silent.

Carsten looked the men over. None of them matched the face on his handbill. "Take those men to the cells. I'll talk to Sheriff Moon."

The saloon was quiet after they herded the trail hands out. Carsten walked over to the bar with Sheriff Moon. The bartender emerged from beneath the counter.

"Any whiskey left?" Carsten asked.

"On the house." The bartender uncorked an intact bottle and poured out two shots.

"Much obliged." Carsten tipped his hat. He clinked glasses with Sheriff Moon. "Now, what can you tell me 'bout Blaine Weber?"

"Not much, I'm afraid," Sheriff Moon replied. "I'd heard he was passin' through here 'bout three weeks ago. But I never saw the fella. Sorry."

"Darn it." Carsten slugged back the whiskey. "Well, if one of those fellas in your hoosegow spills any beans or anythin' just send a wire to my office in Phoenix."

"Will do." Moon shook his hand.

Chapter 7
The Opening Volleys

Norman Reid walked across the compound as a rooster crowed. He approached the house.

Boon sat at his table on the porch with his coffee and breakfast. "Sit down, Mr. Reid." He gestured to the vacant chair. "You want some coffee?"

"No, thanks." Reid sat down. "Have you seen the headlines?" He handed over a copy of the *Daily Phoenix Herald*.

"Bowman Ratcliff gang caught near Phoenix by US Marshals," Boon read aloud. "US Marshal Carsten McNeil apprehended the notorious stagecoach robber in an elaborate scheme to draw out and ensnare his gang, wanted for the robbery of a US Mail carrier."

"Do you think they'll talk?" Reid said. "Just give the word, and I'll ensure he won't. I've heard of Carsten McNeil. He's real fast on the draw, but he's soft. Never wants to kill unless he's made to. But he's also a real cunning lawman."

"I wouldn't worry." Boon took a sip of coffee. "If I thought Ratcliff was going to divulge anything, I wouldn't have sent him away. And even if he did talk, nobody's gonna buy his story. It's safer to just let him be. Don't give this lawman a reason to suspect us. Anyway, I need your talents elsewhere.

With Patterson serving as my partner in this new venture, we should help him remove a stone from our respective boots."

"Frazer?" Reid leaned closer.

"Precisely. I want you to give his family a scare. But make it look like Patterson's behind it. I'd rather those two sheepherders hated each other more than me. So we're going to ignite the kindling and retire to a safe distance in this matter."

"Right, boss." Reid stood up.

"Just don't kill Frazer. I need him and Patterson alive in order to buy their land. Perhaps target his flock. Take Weber and Moony with you."

"Sure thing." Reid nodded.

***

Reid's horse walked along the trail. Blaine Weber, a mustachioed man with shoulder-length hair and worn trail clothes, rode alongside him. Riding opposite was Todd Moony, a larger figure with a bushy beard.

"What's the plan, boss?" Weber asked.

"Put the fear of God into these sheep farmers," Reid said. "Frazer uses this land for grazing his flock, and he ain't got no reason to suspect Patterson of wantin' his land. Drive the flock away. It don't matter where they end up or if any get killed."

"I'm just glad to not be seein' those adobe walls for a spell," Weber said.

"That sounds like ingratitude." Reid glowered at him. "I'd watch that if I was you." He led them up a hill that overlooked a pasture. He dismounted and grabbed a Sharps rifle from his saddle ring.

The bleating of sheep echoed in the distance. He surveyed the area. A flock of sheep milled about in the pasture, accompanied by a single ranch hand.

"What do we do 'bout the fella on watch?" Weber said.

"I'll worry 'bout him." Reid crouched behind a rock and aimed down the rifle's sights. "What are you two starin' at? Get gone. Ride slow 'til you hear the shot."

Weber and Moony led their horses away.

Reid focused his sight on the shepherd. He took a deep breath to steady his aim. He pulled the trigger. The high-caliber rifle shot echoed like thunder. Below, the shepherd lay dead on the ground.

Weber and Moony rode toward the flock at a gallop. They whooped and hollered, firing their guns. The sheep fled. Others rolled across the pasture as the bullets made their mark. Reid stowed the rifle and remounted his horse.

***

"Hoowee!" Weber said as they trotted back along the trail. "That was a fun old ride. Not sure if you really had to kill the shepherd, though."

"Did you want him giving your description to the sheriff?" Reid said.

"I thought he worked for Boon," Weber replied.

"That's *Mister* Boon to you." Reid pointed at Weber, who swallowed. "He can't protect you if you get careless like that. Besides, what are you wanted for?"

"Stealin' horses." Weber looked away from Reid.

"That's a hangin' offense, just the same as murder," Reid said. "It don't matter whether or not you kill someone, you're still gonna swing if you get caught. When you ride with me, we do things my way. Got it?"

Weber nodded. "I just hate feelin' cooped up," he said under his breath.

"What was that?" Reid glared at him.

"I said I was feelin' cooped up at that compound," Weber replied. "I wanted to stretch my legs."

"Nobody leaves the compound without permission." Reid stared into Weber's eyes. "You want whiskey? We've got whiskey. You want cards? We have that too. You want a girl?"

"Four Mexican whores and that redhead girl," Weber said. "But suppose I want some variety?"

Reid brought his horse parallel to Weber's. He booted him from his saddle.

Weber reached for the gun on his belt. Reid drew his Schofield. The click of the hammer prompted Weber to freeze.

"We made you clear of the rules when you first came here." Reid aimed the Schofield at Weber's forehead. "I confine everybody to the compound unless they're workin' the herd or they have permission from Mr. Boon or myself. If you want variety, you can get that from the vultures and the coyotes. Understand?"

Weber nodded. His hand trembled.

"Good." Reid uncocked and holstered his gun. "Now get back on your horse."

Chapter 8
Trouble in Tucson

Three days later, Carsten stared out of a train window. Desert scrub lined the horizon. His deputies sat together in a passenger car.

"Don't worry 'bout losin' Weber." Gibson patted Carsten on the shoulder. "There ain't no sense in spendin' too much time on one man when others are still at large."

"You sound like my old man." Carsten chuckled. "Maybe we should send a letter out like Elfego Baca."

"Would that work?" Wilkins leaned over from the seat in front of Carsten.

"It worked for him," Carsten said. "Sent out a stern letter to all the wanted criminals in Socorro County, and more than half just gave themselves up right then and there. After that shoot-out in Frisco, I don't blame 'em."

"We could use a fella like him ridin' with us," Gibson said.

"Believe me, I've tried." Carsten fanned himself with his hat. "He was a US Marshal, but he retired two years back. He's studyin' law now."

The train's whistle penetrated the dull rattle. Carsten felt a jolt as it slowed down. A cloud of steam surrounded the window.

"Next stop, Tucson!" The conductor made his way through the passenger car.

"This is us, fellas." Carsten stood up with a groan.

The midday sun and the steam made the heat unbearable. Carsten and his deputies stepped onto the platform. He knocked on the window to the ticket booth.

"How can I help you today?" the stationmaster asked.

"I'm lookin' for the best saloons in town," Carsten said.

"If you want somewhere lively, I'd recommend the Dainty Lady." the stationmaster replied. "Just head down the main street after leaving the station until you see the dry goods store on the corner. Follow it around, and you'll see a butcher's shop across the street. It's right next to that. If you're looking for somewhere quieter, just keep heading down that street, and it'll snake its way to an adobe building called the Brass Tack. It'll be right next to the barbershop."

"Much obliged." Carsten tipped his hat and stepped away from the booth. He led his deputies to the livery car, where porters offloaded their horses. Carsten mounted Dan and rode out of the livery yard.

The streets of Tucson were quieter in the afternoon as people looked for shade. The horses rode at a walking pace along the dusty street. Carsten passed a stagecoach being loaded outside the local company's depot. He noticed the dry goods store pointed out by the stationmaster. He turned the corner. A bearded man in a bloodstained apron dozed on the porch in front of a house across the street. A meat cleaver lay embedded on a table in front of him.

"Wilkins," Carsten said, "you and Brennan check out the Brass Tack. Gibson and Nastas, you're with me. We'll search the Dainty Lady."

The deputies nodded in agreement. Wilkins and Moses rode down the street. Carsten hitched his horse outside the two-story clapboard structure next to the butcher's shop. Several bullet holes dotted the porch above the sign, including the i in "Dainty." He heard chatter emanating from within.

"Best stow the stars, boys." Carsten removed his badge and put it in his pocket. "This place might be rough. You get a look at our men's faces?"

"Alvin McIntyre and Mitchel Winn?" Gibson asked as Nastas replied with a curt nod.

"Those are the ones," Carsten said. "Keep your eyes and ears open for any faces or talk. If they're in there, we may not be able to bring 'em in without difficulty."

The interior of the saloon contrasted the subdued atmosphere of outside. Two trail hands arm wrestled on one table, grunting at the exertion. Two miners played five-finger fillet on another, their knives providing a staccato as they pockmarked the table. Some patrons stared at the newcomers.

Carsten walked to an unoccupied space at the bar. "Three beers." He placed two dimes on the table.

"I don't serve Indians." The bartender pointed at Nastas.

"Give them what they want." A cowboy standing beside Carsten inched away from him. "I know this fella, and there might be difficulty if'n he's rebuffed."

Carsten tensed.

"You do?" The bartender's eyebrow raised.

"I think this fella has mistaken me for somebody else," Carsten said.

"Ain't no mistake," the cowboy said. "That there is Carsten McNeil."

The chatter fell silent. Some patrons inched away. Others made a move toward the door. Gibson and Nastas scanned the room.

"I'm sorry, Mr. McNeil." The bartender trembled. "You and your friends are welcome."

Carsten ignored the sound of the beers pouring into glasses. He focused his gaze on a corner table, where two men stared back at him. He saw one of them fidgeting. The man had shaggy black hair protruding from beneath his hat.

"How is it you've heard of me?" Carsten asked with a smile as he took his beer.

"From that difficulty in the courthouse in Phoenix," the man said.

"Come to think of it," Carsten replied, "you look familiar too."

"I get that a lot." The cowboy downed his whiskey. "I gotta get back on the trail. It was nice talkin' to ya."

"Hold it." Carsten grabbed his arm. "Your face is real familiar, Mitchel Winn."

The cowboy froze. He eyed his gun.

"Don't try it." Carsten wagged a finger. "I'll put in a good word with the judge for you if'n you tell me where your friend Alvin McIntyre is. But if you resist, you'll be on your own. Shoot me or any of my deputies, and you'll face a rope."

Mitchel looked toward a table in the far corner. A man with a bushy moustache stood up and drew a revolver.

"Carsten, look out!" Gibson lunged forward.

A shot rang out. Somebody screamed. Gibson stumbled to the floor. Carsten drew his Remington and returned fire. Gun smoke filled the room. The gunman fell onto the table, tipping it over. Glass smashed as a whiskey bottle rolled onto the floor. Carsten turned back to Mitchel and cocked his gun. The outlaw raised his hands.

"Nastas, check on Gibson." Carsten removed Mitchel's gun from its holster. "Mitchel Winn, you're under arrest for stagecoach robbery. Everyone else calm down. We ain't gonna shoot nobody unless they shoot us."

The saloon doors swung open.

"We heard shootin'!" Wilkins stepped inside with one of his revolvers drawn. Moses entered close behind, shotgun in hand.

"We've got Winn," Carsten said. "But Gibson's been hit. Check the other body. I reckon that was McIntyre. Brennan, see to Winn."

Moses advanced on Mitchel, keeping his shotgun trained on him. Carsten kneeled over Gibson. The deputy sat against the bar. He clutched a bleeding wound in his stomach. His breathing was labored. Nastas looked at Carsten and shook his head.

"The other fella's McIntyre," Wilkins called out. "He's dead."

Three men entered the saloon, armed with rifles. "Drop your weapons!"

Carsten noticed badges on their shirts. "I'm a US Marshal," Carsten replied. "We've got one fella in custody, one for the undertaker, and one of our men is gut-shot." He stood up and removed his badge from his pocket.

"Who are they?" the sheriff asked.

"That there's Mitchel Winn." Carsten gestured to Winn, whom Moses had handcuffed. "The dead fella over there is Alvin McIntyre. They're wanted for a stagecoach robbery up near Bisbee. I have arrest warrants for them signed by Federal Judge Arma Stanley in Phoenix. I suggest you wire him if you still wish to confirm my identity."

"Who's the fella who's been hit?" The sheriff lowered his gun.

"Deputy Marshal Jack Gibson," Carsten said.

"Marshal," Gibson said, "any chance of a cigar?"

Carsten snapped his fingers for the bartender, who removed one from the display case on the bar. He handed him a nickel and took the cigar. He sat beside Gibson and placed the cigar in his mouth. Gibson nodded. Carsten struck a match on the side of the bar to light it.

"I swore off these when I married Rowena," Gibson said in a weak voice. "Really missed them."

"I'm sorry I got you into this," Carsten said.

"It ain't your fault." Gibson reached for the cigar. "You think I would have made marshal?"

"You were one of the best." Carsten nodded.

Gibson smiled. He exhaled and closed his eyes.

"You bastard!" Moses yelled. A thump and a grunt followed.

Carsten stood up. He saw Moses strike Mitchel in the stomach with the butt of his shotgun.

"That's enough!" Carsten said. "He's surrendered, and he didn't shoot Gibson."

Moses backed away from Carsten's glare.

Carsten turned to the sheriff and his deputies. "I'm gonna need to hold this man in your cell until we can take the next train back to Phoenix."

***

Carsten sat in front of the desk in the sheriff's office. A glass of whiskey sat untouched in front of him. Wilkins, Moses, and Nastas loitered in the office with two of the deputies. Mitchel lay on the wooden cot in one cell.

"I heard a great deal 'bout you, Marshal McNeil." One deputy patted him on the shoulder. "My name's John, and my partner there is Steve. The fella down at the telegraph office is Ben."

"Nice to meet y'all," Carsten said.

"What do you want us to do 'bout your deputy?" Steve asked.

"He's goin' back with us," Carsten said. "He's got a wife back in Phoenix, and I reckon it's only right he gets buried there. I gotta break that to her."

"This is the career we all picked," John said. "Some of us are married. Some of us ain't. Losin' a partner in the line of duty ain't an easy thing. It's just as hard as takin' a life."

"I had to take lives when I was still between hay and grass," Carsten said. "Some brothers of a man my pa killed in the line of duty wanted to get revenge after he'd retired. They could have killed my whole family if we didn't."

"Like Billy the Kid?" Steve asked. "The fella who killed twenty-one people before he was twenty one?"

"That always sounded like a tall yarn," Carsten said, "but I ain't gonna argue 'bout what happened and what didn't."

"Why not?" John asked. "I've heard many stories 'bout your battle against Alphonse Moraday and your fight with John Garrett. Whether or not they're true, they sound real amazing."

"I don't think so," Carsten said. "I don't believe in celebratin' my exploits. There isn't much to gain from it.

"You could put it in a book and make a ton of money from it," John said.

"I could." Carsten nodded. "But I don't want to. I'm lookin' at retirin' from the lawman business. I got a wife as well, and she's gonna worry 'bout me. If my exploits get published, that'll bring me too much attention. I've had plenty of folks comin' after me to prove their mettle already."

The door to the office opened. Ben stepped inside. "Just had a response from the judge's office. They've confirmed who you are and who your quarries are. Or were. They've said to report back as soon as you return to Phoenix."

"Much obliged." Carsten tipped his hat. "Can we hold them here until the next train arrives?"

Chapter 9
Cabin Fever

Blaine Weber lay in Amy Filmore's bed. He stared at the ceiling while she got dressed. "I'm sick of this damn compound. All the liquor's watered down, and I'm havin' fun with the same five girls. And that's if'n I'm lucky not to have to wait all night." A hammering on the door prompted him to sit up.

"Open up!" someone outside shouted. "It's my turn with Miss Filmore."

"Son of a…" Blaine heaved himself out of the bed. He grabbed a shirt. Amy threw him his pants. He put them on and grabbed a shirt.

"Hurry up in there!" the voice outside shouted.

Blaine grabbed his hat and boots. He opened the door. Another man pushed past him to enter the room. Blaine stepped into the bar area of Boon's Cantina. Todd Moony and four others sat around one table, engrossed in a poker game.

"Hey, Blaine!" Todd waved to him. "You in?"

"What's the buy-in?" Blaine slumped into a vacant chair.

"One dollar." One of the ranch hands, Lyle, cut the deck.

"Good thing I didn't pay for any longer with Amy." Blaine reached into his pocket and felt a folded paper.

"Lookin' for somethin'?" Todd said.

"Some of these coins are slippery." Blaine scattered a handful of loose change onto the table. He counted them up. "That should amount to a dollar."

The ranch hand nodded. He scooped up the coins and replaced them with a stack of chips.

"How are things outside?" Blaine asked.

"Not good." Lyle sighed. "A fella broke his leg after fallin' off his horse today."

"Do you need another hand?" Blaine said. "I feel I might as well make myself useful while I'm stayin' here."

"I'd be much obliged." Lyle grinned. "We start at dawn, right after breakfast."

"Are we gonna play some cards or apply for more jobs?" Todd asked.

***

The cook's bell roused Blaine from his sleep the following morning. He followed the other trail hands out of the bunkhouse. The camp's cook stirred a large Dutch oven over a fire by his chuck wagon. Blaine helped himself to some coffee from the nearby pot.

"We'll be headin' out to pasture to watch the herd," Lyle said. "I can loan you a horse if you need one. You can pay me back from that pot you won last night."

"Much obliged," Blaine said. He took a plate of beans from the cook and sat down away from the other hands.

Once done, Blaine stuck his empty plate and coffee cup in the washbasin. Lyle approached him. The ranch hand led two horses from the barn. Blaine mounted the horse. He followed the other men at a walking pace toward the compound gates. The two guards pulled the gates open and the ranch hands broke into a trot.

"So, what's the plan for today?" Blaine asked.

"We're checkin' the herd to make sure the pasture's still fit for grazin'," Lyle replied. "We also need to make sure anybody passin' through here pays the toll. I figure that's somethin' you could be useful for."

"Like those fellas?" Blaine pointed at three riders coming up the trail with a flock of sheep.

"Probably gonna be Patterson or Frazer hands," Lyle replied. "Let's find out. Let me do the jawin'. If'n they don't pony up the toll, threaten to scatter the sheep. That usually works."

Blaine followed Lyle toward the flock. One rider moved ahead of the flock to meet them. He had white hair and a thin beard.

"Good mornin', Mr. Frazer," Lyle said. "Where are you takin' them woolies today?"

"The pasture," Frazer said. "Someone sent some men to drive off my herd last week. Patterson, by my reckoning."

"Well, this here is Mr. Boon's land," Lyle said. "It's gonna cost you five bucks to drive your sheep through here."

Blaine rested his hand on his holster.

"Fine." Frazer reached into his pocket. He handed five silver dollars to Lyle.

"Much obliged." Lyle tipped his hat. "Now get movin'. Last thing I want is those sheep spookin' our cattle."

***

By late afternoon, Blaine winced. His body ached all over. He trotted around the edges of Boon's herd and looked around. The rest of the trail crew had spread out. He turned his horse around, toward another trail leading to Rockbed.

"I ain't cut out for this," he muttered under his breath as he looked over his shoulder.

The other trail hands rode the edges of the herd as they milled about the pastureland. Blaine turned away from them and loped down the trail.

The sun set as Blaine arrived in Rockbed. He hitched his horse outside the saloon. Piano music emanated from within. He smiled.

Blaine sauntered into the saloon. Most of the tables sat vacant, except for one taken up by three old-timers with a deck of cards. Another man sat alone by the door with a newspaper. Two women in cheap dresses leaned over a mezzanine balcony. They waved fans and smiled at Blaine. He tipped his hat to them and walked over to the bar.

"I ain't seen you 'round here before." The bartender looked him over. "What can I get for you, stranger?"

"Just passin' through," Blaine said. "I'll have a beer and a shot of whiskey to chase it up."

"That'll be fifteen cents," the bartender replied.

"Place seems fairly quiet." Blaine scattered coins on the counter.

"It's early yet." The bartender poured a beer into a glass. "I get the hired hands from the Patterson and Frazer ranches, but I heard Mr. Boon has his own cantina on his ranch. But I say thank God since that's one less bunch of roostered cowboys causing trouble in my place. Speaking of which..." He pointed to a sign above the bar that said *No Firearms*.

Blaine removed his gun belt and handed it over.

The bartender handed him his beer.

"Much obliged." Blaine leaned on the counter and sipped the beer for a bit.

He set the empty beer glass down and picked up his whiskey. The doors to the saloon swung open. Three men in trail clothes stepped inside. Their spurs clinked as they approached the bar. One of them bumped into Blaine. He gripped his whiskey glass. Some of its contents spilled onto the bar.

"Whiskeys all around," one man said.

His friends piled their guns onto the bar. The bartender nodded. He set out glasses and poured the whiskey across them.

"I think I'll take another whiskey too." Blaine slugged the contents of his glass and held it out.

"Who's talkin' to you, mister?" One of the ranch hands grabbed his shoulder.

"Take your hand off me." Blaine looked ahead at the glasses on the bar.

"You think you can drink with us, but you don't have the decency to look at me when I'm talkin' to you?" The trail hand yanked his shoulder. "Who are you anyway?"

"Maybe he's one of Patterson's boys," one of the other ranch hands said.

"Yeah," the third added. "They've been givin' us trouble lately."

"Let's get some payback, boys!" the first man yelled. "Grab him!"

The bartender ducked behind the counter. Blaine wrenched free of the man's grasp and snatched the abandoned whiskey bottle. Another man grabbed him, pinioning his arms. The first man punched him in the stomach. The second man wrenched the bottle out of his hand.

Blaine kicked upward. The bottle flew out of his assailant's hand and shattered against the floor. He pushed his feet against the bar. They both tumbled back and his grappler slammed against a nearby table. The man's grip loosened, so Blaine elbowed him in the face.

The third man delivered a left hook. Blaine spat out a broken tooth. He tackled the man. The first kicked him in the ribs. Blaine tumbled over. He covered his face and groin as the two men kicked and punched him.

One of them reached into his pocket. "Hey, he's got a love letter here!" He unfolded the paper and laughed.

"We'll read it later," the other said. "Put it away and keep hittin' him."

A shot rang out behind them.

"That's enough!" Willie Snow stood in the doorway, holding a smoking pistol. "Step away from that man. You're under arrest."

Two of the men stood up and raised their hands. The third just lay there, silent.

"Thanks, sheriff." Blaine scrambled to his feet. "I'd best be goin'."

"You ain't goin' nowhere." Snow aimed the revolver at him. "I just had a report that you stole this fella's horse.

Stealin' horses is a hangin' offense last time I checked, so you'd best have a real good explanation."

Lyle stepped into the saloon behind the sheriff. He scowled at Blaine. "That's him," he said. "I loaned him a horse so he could work the herd, and he went into town without permission."

"I only borrowed the horse," Blaine said. "I was gonna give it back. I was tired of bein' cooped up in that compound."

"Save it," Lyle said. "Mr. Boon will hear of this. Thank you, Sheriff. I'll take him back to the ranch. Unless you need help takin' those Frazer boys in for causin' a fracas."

"Much obliged," Snow replied. "But I've got two fellas who can carry their friend to the cells. You'd best take this fella back. I reckon Mr. Boon will want to speak with him."

The two ranch hands picked up the third. They draped him over their shoulders and walked outside. Snow followed behind with his gun trained on all three of them.

"Come on, you." Lyle grabbed Blaine by the collar. "Outside. Pronto."

Blaine stumbled onto the street as Lyle shoved him through the doors. He brushed trail dust away and scrambled to his feet. Reid glowered at him from atop his horse. Todd loitered by the hitching post.

"Oh damn…" Blaine said.

"Hogtie him," Reid said with a cutting tone.

Todd grabbed Blaine and pinned him to the floor. Lyle grabbed a length of rope from his saddle. He bound his hands and feet. Once secured, Todd lifted Blaine up and stowed him atop the recovered horse. He and Lyle mounted their own horses and followed Reid out.

***

Night had fallen by the time the procession returned to the Boon compound. Todd removed Blaine from the horse and dropped him to the ground in the yard. A bell emanated from the porch, prompting ranch hands to emerge from the bunkhouse and the cantina.

Boon strode into the yard. "Mr. Weber, isn't it?"

Blaine spat on the ground by his feet.

"You have a lot of explaining to do," Boon continued. "You borrowed a horse from one of my hands and used it to go into Rockbed and cause trouble. I made it quite clear when you first arrived that the town is off-limits to everyone here. You're a wanted felon, like many men here, and your actions could have endangered all their lives and cost me a workforce. Why?"

"I just wanted to go into town." Tears welled in Blaine's eyes. "I was feelin' cooped up and irritable."

"But I have a cantina." Boon raised his voice. "That's open to any of my employees. I took you in and shielded you from the law. I offered you entertainment and this is how you repay me?"

"I'm sorry, Mr. Boon," Blaine stammered. "It won't happen again."

"You're right, Mr. Weber." Boon produced a Webley Bulldog from his jacket pocket. "It won't." He pressed the gun into Blaine's temple.

Blaine shut his eyes.

"Let this be a lesson for everybody watching!" Boon shouted. "Nobody leaves this compound without permission. Too many lives are at stake. This will happen to anybody who disobeys from this point onward."

The shot echoed through the compound.

Chapter 10
A Train to Yuma

A week later, Carsten sat in the stuffy courtroom. Bowman Ratcliff and his three accomplices sat handcuffed at the defendant's table.

"Mr. Foreman." Judge Stanley turned to the jury box. "How do you find the accused?"

"Guilty, your honor," the juror replied, and Carsten smiled.

"Bowman Ratcliff." The judge turned to the defendants. "This court finds you and your accomplices guilty of stagecoach robbery. I hereby sentence the four of you to twenty years at Yuma Territorial Prison. I adjourn this court." He struck his gavel.

Carsten watched deputies escort the gang out of the courtroom. He noticed Fleur smiling in the gallery. He left the building with the other people watching the sentencing. Outside the courtroom, Carsten embraced Fleur.

"I met with Rowena Gibson this morning," she said.

"Is she copin' all right?" Carsten asked. "It's been two days since the funeral."

"As well as the rest of us," Fleur replied.

"Jack Gibson was a good deputy. He took a bullet to save me. I owe him more than I can give."

"I've been thinking about what you said." Tears welled in Fleur's eyes. "You talked about Gibson being your successor. What will happen now?"

"My term finishes soon," Carsten said. "And we will go back to Prescott when that happens."

"Marshal McNeil." The bailiff tapped him on the shoulder. "Judge Stanley wants to speak with you in his chambers."

"Duty calls, darlin'." Carsten let go of Fleur. "I'll speak to you again later."

***

Carsten sat down in a chair in front of Judge Stanley's desk.

"Would you like a drink?" Judge Stanley walked over to a liquor cabinet in the corner of his chambers.

"No thanks," Carsten said.

The judge took his seat and stared at Carsten, but with a softer gaze. "I'm sorry about Gibson. Losing a marshal in the line of duty is never easy to deal with, but sometimes it's inevitable. Gibson knew the risks. So did your father. So do you."

"Yes, your honor." Carsten nodded.

"I know what you're going to say. But imagine if that was Fleur who took a bullet for you. Could you forgive yourself, then?"

"I guess not. But with that in mind, wouldn't she have known the risks as well?"

"I suppose she would have," Stanley replied. "But she's your wife. It's not right for a man to put his wife at risk. She could be killed in just the same way as Gibson. And then where would you be?"

"You didn't get him killed," Carsten said.

"And neither did you, so don't beat yourself up about it. You're still a US Marshal, and I can't afford to have you feeling sorry for yourself. I will see that Mrs. Gibson is taken care of. But you have your warrants to serve. Are you still up to the task?"

Carsten nodded.

"Excellent." The judge sat back. "I'm going to need you to deliver Ratcliff and his gang to Yuma today. Train's at ten past three. Can you handle that?"

"Yes, your honor."

"It can give you time to think about things. Perhaps Blaine Weber may show himself while you're away. Then you can track him down and bring him in. While you were away, a fella wanted for robbing a general store turned himself in."

"Really?" Carsten raised an eyebrow.

"I'm not kidding. When he heard about the arrest warrant, he came by the office and surrendered. He thought you were going to track him down."

Carsten was still shaking his head in disbelief when he left the judge's chamber.

Fleur sat on the seat outside. "Everything all right?" She stood up.

"I'm gonna be headin' to Yuma this afternoon. Prisoner transfer."

"Right." Fleur looked down at the floor. "I'll check on Rowena. See if she needs anything."

"I'm sorry I'm not around," Carsten said. "I'm also sorry I can't deputize you. But the judge said somethin' that's gnawin' at me."

"He made you suppose if I was in Gibson's place?" Fleur asked.

"That's too good to be a guess." Carsten tilted his head, his eyes asking for more.

"I've come to know the judge's thoughts these past few weeks," Fleur said. "And Rowena talked about it, too. It's fine. I think I'm understanding."

Carsten nodded.

***

The early afternoon sun bore down on the station platform. Carsten rested a shotgun on his lap. He hunched on the bench, trying to take advantage of what little shade was on offer. He stepped inside the station building to see Ratcliff and his gang on one bench in the waiting area, manacled together. Wilkins, Moses, and Nastas stood in the corners, their weapons trained on the prisoners.

"We gonna be waitin' much longer?" Wilkins asked.

Carsten checked his pocket watch. It was half-past three. "It's twenty minutes late."

"I hate waitin' on trains," Moses said.

"I do too." Carsten fidgeted. "Sickens me they make folk pay through the nose for service like that."

"Amen," Wilkins said.

"That's why I never felt bad robbin' them." Ratcliff grinned. "Railroads steal more in a year than I ever could in one day."

His men laughed at the remark.

"You shut your mouth!" Wilkins barked at him. "You're lucky you didn't kill nobody on your heists. Else the judge would have made you swing."

Carsten stepped over to the ticket booth. "Any news on the Yuma train?"

"I ain't heard nothin'." The clerk shrugged. "No wires have been sent, so it probably wasn't held up."

"Thanks anyhow," Carsten said.

"Sooner it arrives, the sooner we get our waiting area back," the clerk replied.

A whistle echoed in the distance. Carsten peered outside to see a train approach the platform. "That looks like ours," he said. "Get 'em on their feet and get 'em outside."

"You heard the marshal!" Wilkins said. "Move it!"

The prisoners stood up. The rattle of their chains echoed through the waiting area.

Carsten stepped outside. He opened the double doors. Several onlookers peered inside. "Please keep clear," he said to them. "We're transportin' prisoners."

The bystanders pressed against the walls or stepped away from the double doors. Moses backed out with his shotgun at the ready. The Ratcliff gang stepped onto the platform. Carsten trained his shotgun on them as he gestured for them to move to the far end of the platform.

The train ground to a halt, letting out another whistle. Carsten directed his prisoners to a reinforced boxcar near the caboose. A porter slid the door open to reveal a cage inside. Carsten stepped inside. Two other deputies occupied the car. One of them moved to unlock the cage.

"Rusty and Lancaster, reportin' for duty," one deputy said.

"All right," Carsten said. "Let's get 'em inside."

The prisoners scrambled up into the car. The two deputies ushered them into the cage while Carsten maintained his aim. Moses and Nastas clambered in. Nastas set down his rifle to help Wilkins up. Rusty locked the cage.

"We're all on, Marshal," Wilkins said.

Carsten gave a thumb up to the porter, who shut the door. The train car had no windows, and a series of hanging lanterns provided the only light. They cast shadows across the interior of the car.

A few moments later, another whistle sounded, and the train lurched ahead. Carsten sat against the wall of the boxcar, removed his hat and used it to fan himself.

"Mind if I join you?" Lancaster asked.

Carsten gestured to the space next to him.

Lancaster sat down. "I heard a great deal 'bout you. That business with the gunman in the courthouse was amazin'."

Carsten smiled and nodded.

"Everythin' all right, Marshal?" Wilkins asked.

"Just thinkin'," Carsten replied.

"What about?" Lancaster asked.

"A felon who disappeared," Carsten said. "I think his handle was Blaine Weber. He was last seen in Florence a couple of weeks back, but the trail went cold. Even Nastas couldn't track him. It was like he just vanished like some backward miracle."

"Blaine Weber?" Ratcliff said. "He went to ground with us a while back."

Carsten's eyes widened. He stood up and marched over to the cage. "You knew Blaine Weber? I never knew he rode with you."

"He didn't," Ratcliff said. "He just went to ground with us."

"Where was this?" Carsten said.

"That's somethin' I ain't sharin'." Ratcliff wagged a finger.

"I can speak to the judge," Carsten said. "You tell me where you hid, and maybe I can get your sentences reduced."

"Forget it, Marshal." Ratcliff sat back against the cage with his arms folded. "You're dealin' with someone mighty powerful. If I talk, they'll know. Whether I'm holed up in Yuma or I walk free, I'm gonna be killed."

"You mean someone took over John Garrett's operation?" Carsten said.

"I guess." Ratcliff shrugged.

"Basically, did you answer to a fella who called himself el Presidente?" Carsten leaned against the cage.

"Not since you busted him," Ratcliff said. "Go ahead. Beat it outta me. I heard 'bout you."

Carsten stepped back. "There was another deputy I rode with who went by the name of Nash. He was a real fire-and-brimstone type who was known for bein' a real curly wolf to those in his custody."

"So?" Ratcliff grinned.

"I ain't him," Carsten said. "And I ain't gonna become him." He stepped away from the cage and sat down against the wall of the boxcar.

The sound of gunshots outside prompted Carsten to stand up. The train jerked to a halt. Carsten pressed against the wall to keep upright.

"What the hell?" Rusty grabbed his rifle. "Someone tryin' to rob the train or spring the prisoners?"

"You wouldn't know anythin' 'bout this, would you?" Carsten stared at Ratcliff, who shrugged in response.

"Worry 'bout it later." Wilkins drew and cocked one of his revolvers.

"Everybody get down!" Carsten yelled.

More shots echoed outside. He heard the metallic pings of bullets as they ricocheted against the boxcar, unable to penetrate it.

"Who's out there?" Carsten shouted as the shots wound down.

"This is a holdup!" a voice outside yelled. "Open the door and throw out your guns!"

"We ain't carryin' anythin' of value!" Carsten replied. "This is a prisoner transport."

"I don't believe you," the robber shouted. "If you don't open the door pronto, we'll dynamite it. You have until the count of ten. One!"

"Any ideas, Marshal?" Lancaster whispered.

"I'm thinkin', I'm thinkin'," Carsten replied.

"Two!"

"We can open the doors and let them have it," Rusty hissed.

"Three!"

"We don't know how many are out there," Carsten replied.

"Four!"

"We'll have to risk it." Lancaster tightened his grip on his rifle.

"They might have taken the passengers hostage," Carsten said.

"Five!"

"I'll go out," Carsten said. "I'll see how many there are. Keep outta sight and wait for my signal."

"Six!"

"What's the signal?" Wilkins asked.

"Seven!"

"Our usual one," Carsten said, and Wilkins nodded.

"Eight!"

"Okay!" Carsten yelled. "We're comin' out!"

Lancaster unlocked the padlock on the boxcar door and slid it open. Carsten gripped his repeater by the barrel. He held it out of the doorway. He peered outside. Six masked men stood near the door.

Carsten set the rifle down and jumped out of the boxcar. He raised his hands and walked toward the robbers. "My name is US Marshal Carsten McNeil. Maybe y'all have heard of me. Maybe you haven't. But I'll tell you right here and now that you're makin' a big mistake. Ride on, and I'll let this slide for now. But if'n you don't, it's your choice of lead or the rope."

"You're Quaker McNeil?" one robber said.

"So you've heard of me?" Carsten grinned.

"Be quiet!" the spokesperson growled at his subordinate. He turned back to Carsten. "I got two more men in the passenger cars takin' valuables. You don't want any of those folks gettin' hurt, now do you? I heard all about Stan Whitmore. I'm callin' you out."

"Tell your people in the passenger cars to come out here," Carsten said. "Then I'll accept."

"Let me check your express car," the gang leader said. He gestured for two of his men, who walked over to the boxcar.

"My men are still in there." Carsten raised his voice. "You can look, and they won't shoot."

"Anything happens to them, you die." The robber pointed his gun at Carsten's forehead. He cocked it.

Carsten maintained his stare on him.

"The marshal ain't lyin' boss!" one robber called from within the boxcar. "There's no safe. Just four guys in a cage!"

"You can still walk away," Carsten said.

"No," the robber said. "I want to see how fast you really are. After all, if I'm the fella who has killed Quaker McNeil, I'll be feared throughout the territory."

"You will be," Carsten said. "But be ready to deal with folks thinkin' the same thing."

Once all the robbers stepped off the train, they watched their leader face Carsten. The deputies stood beside them, weapons at the ready. Carsten stared down the leader. He took a breath.

"Draw." The leader reached for his gun.

Carsten drew his Remington and fired.

The robber looked down. His pistol fell to the ground with a clatter as he slumped forward.

Carsten turned to the rest of the gang. "Unless you want to end up like him, you'd best walk away."

One man reached for his gun. A shot rang out. He slumped against the carriage. The other robbers stepped away. Nastas held a smoking pistol and nodded to Carsten.

"Anyone else?" Carsten looked around.

The other bandits scattered.

"Leave the loot," Carsten shouted to a pair of robbers carrying sacks.

They set them down and ran to their horses. Carsten walked over and kicked dust over the dead man's face. As the robbers rode away, the passengers on the train applauded Carsten. Lancaster and Rusty walked up and patted him on the back.

"Nice work, Marshal," Lancaster said. "I thought we were done for."

"Well, I figured those robbers weren't the brightest bunch, tryin' to hold up a train to Yuma," Carsten replied. "Well done for keepin' your head."

"I thought they would have tried to spring Ratcliff," Rusty said with a grin.

"I thought so too." Carsten nodded in agreement. "Did he or his boys do anythin' when the robbers boarded the car?"

Rusty shook his head.

"Then we could rule that out as a motive," Carsten said. "I guess we caught all of 'em with that initial trap."

***

Carsten looked at his pocket watch as the train continued to rattle along. He held it toward the light. Seven o'clock. He produced a paper bag of beef jerky from his pocket and chewed on a piece. Ratcliff and his accomplices sat in the cage and watched him.

"There ain't much left, but help yourselves." He pushed the packet through the cage bars.

The captives moved to grab the packet. Ratcliff aimed a glance at them. They backed away. The gang leader took the packet and shared the contents between his three men.

"Thanks, Carsten." Ratcliff gave a thankful nod. "I guess this'll be a luxury compared to whatever grub they serve in jail."

"You mentioned you and Weber went to ground together," Carsten said. "I know you're gonna be tight-lipped 'bout it, but I might as well ask again since there ain't much else to do on this trip."

"You know what?" Ratcliff chuckled. "You ain't gonna believe it anyhow."

"Try me," Carsten said.

"We stayed at a compound in Pleasant Valley," Ratcliff said. "Complete with an in-house cantina and brothel. But it ain't a great selection of girls though. Just four Mexicans and one redhead between everyone stayin' there. Place had the makings of a robber's paradise."

"You're right," Carsten said. "I don't believe you."

Another whistle sounded from the locomotive.

Carsten stood up and readied his shotgun. "Sounds like we're almost there. Get 'em up."

The train rolled to a halt. The door to the boxcar slid open. Carsten winced as light from the setting sun poured inside.

Wilkins stepped out of the boxcar and drew one of his revolvers. "Wagon's here, Marshal!"

Lancaster unlocked the cage. Carsten trained his shotgun on the prisoners as they marched out of the boxcar. Carsten followed them to a horse-drawn prison wagon waiting at the station. A uniformed guard sat in the driver's seat. Another held the door open. Carsten led the gang into the back of the wagon.

The guard locked the door behind him. "Thanks, Marshal," he said. "We'll take them from here."

Carsten nodded.

The guard clambered into the seat next to the driver. He flicked the reins, and the wagon rolled away.

"If you don't mind me sayin'…" Lancaster stood beside Carsten as he watched the wagon leave. "You seemed kinda soft on those prisoners. Not what I expected from a gunfighter of your reputation."

Carsten looked around. Nastas, Wilkins, and Moses glared at the new deputy.

"Might not be a thing to be askin' about," Rusty whispered in his friend's ear.

"I didn't mean no offense." Lancaster raised his hands. "If you don't wanna talk 'bout it, I ain't gonna press further."

"That's wise," Carsten said. "But surely you folks have been stationed near the prison for a while. Haven't you heard people refer to me as Quaker McNeil?"

"I have," Lancaster said. "And I've always wondered why."

"First time I got into a gun fight," Carsten said, "I shot my opponent in the hand. It was a lucky shot. And the big bug who put him up to it built a story on that fact. You know, 'he shot that fella in the hand rather than shootin' to kill, so he must be a Quaker.' You know how that kinda thing travels. But I'd sworn an oath to my pa that I'd never start no gunfight. An enemy may have chosen that handle, but I stuck with it. It kinda suited me."

Lancaster raised his eyebrows and nodded.

"Anyhow," Carsten said. "We'd best find a place to spend the night 'fore the next train back to Phoenix. My deputies and me have a hankerin' for some decent grub. Drinks are on me. I got plenty more stories to share, but it ain't easy without a whiskey in hand."

His deputies gave affirmative murmurs.

"That sounds like a plan." Lancaster exchanged a nod with Rusty. "We know just the place."

"What do you reckon 'bout what Ratcliff was sayin'?" Carsten asked as they walked into the nearby town.

"I ain't got an opinion on that," Lancaster said. "He'd say anythin' to get less time in the hoosegow."

"I reckon you're right," Carsten replied. "I heard there's a place in Nevada where a lot of wanted folk like to go to ground."

"You mean in Las Vegas Valley?" Rusty said. "You try to go there, you'd best put a down payment on a coffin. For you and all your deputies. You'd be sellin' your horse to the vultures halfway there."

"Just a thought," Carsten said. "If some of these outlaws are goin' to ground, I figured it would be somewhere in this territory."

Chapter 11
Range War

As the sun rose, Hank and Aaron loped toward the pasturelands with four other ranch hands.

"Keep up, son," Hank said. "I'm hearin' things are escalatin' in Rockbed. A couple of Frazer's hired hands got into a punch-up at the saloon the other week after they mistook a saddle tramp for one of our hands."

"Was the fella all right?" Aaron asked.

"I doubt it," Hank said. "Snow arrested him for stealin' a horse from one of Mr. Boon's hands. Delivered him straight to Reid. I've heard bad things 'bout that fella."

Aaron gulped.

The riders arrived at the pasture, finding it deserted, save for one or two sheep milling around. Hank froze.

"Where's the flock, Pa?" Aaron said.

"I don't know, son. Surely they'd still be millin' about. They can't have wandered off too far unless..."

"Unless?"

"Someone must have driven them off." Hank tightened his grip on the reins.

"Son of a—" Aaron said.

"Language!" Hank snapped. He took a deep breath. "Come on. Let's see if we can't pick up the trail. See where they've been driven off to." He walked his horse over to a patch of chewed grass.

The hoof prints led to the north. Some came from sheep. Others came from horses.

"Looks like they went this way." Hank said. "I figure some riders drove them away."

"You reckon it was Frazer?" Aaron said.

"I reckon. Round up any sheep you can find and keep behind me. I'll see if there are more ahead. We'll gather them at Cottonwood Creek. If we're lucky, a few of them will be drinkin' there." He turned to the four ranch hands. "Two of you stay with Aaron. The rest of you ride with me."

Hank surveyed the pasture as he followed the flock's tracks. He found more sheep milling along the trail. Two riders rode at a trot from the opposite direction. Hank tightened his grip on the reins. He recognized one of them as Lyle, the trail hand who demanded a toll from him.

"Howdy!" Lyle said as they approached. He gestured for Hank to stop.

"Good mornin'," Hank replied in a noncommittal tone.

"What's your business 'round here, Bo-peep?" Lyle asked.

"My flock's been driven off the pasture," Hank replied. "You seen anythin' out here?"

"Like what?" Lyle shrugged. "The cattle rarely go to that stretch of pasture. There ain't enough decent grass to fill them. That's why Mr. Boon offers it for the woolies."

"So you wouldn't know anythin' 'bout what happened?" Hank stared at Lyle.

"You'd best not be finger-pointin' at us, mister." Lyle's eyes narrowed. "What are accusin' us of?"

"I ain't accusin'." Hank sighed. "I'm just wonderin' if you seen any sheep milling around on your land. Somebody must have driven my flock off the pasture, and a few could've ended up elsewhere on your spread."

Lyle exchanged a glance with the other trail hand, who shrugged. "We'll keep an eye out. But don't get upset if they've been trampled. You know how big them steers are compared to the woolies."

"Fine," Hank said. "I gotta find the bulk of the flock, and then I'll be gone." He tipped his hat and continued down the trail.

"You'd best make sure them woolies don't muddy our herd's waterin' holes," Lyle said behind him. "Or else Mr. Boon will be askin' to be comped."

"I'd better get that cattle from all this," Hank said underneath his breath as he walked his horse away from the two ranch hands.

"What's happenin', Pa?" Aaron rode up toward Hank.

"Nothin'. Why aren't you roundin' up the stragglers?"

"I found a couple and gathered them at the creek like you asked," Aaron replied. "But I saw you with some men and wondered what was happenin'. Ain't they Mr. Boon's hands?"

"It's nothin'," Hank said again. "You watch over the sheep we found so far. I'm gonna find the rest of the flock. It looks like we're gonna be here all day."

"Dammit," Aaron said under his breath.

"I heard that," Hank snarled. "I ain't happy 'bout it neither. Tonight, I will head into Rockbed to ask Frazer about it. But right now, we gotta deal with this. And I'd take it as a kindness if you went 'bout this without cussin' or blasphemin'. Or else you're gonna be outside a whole while longer. Understood?"

"Yes, sir." Aaron nodded.

"I'm glad. Now, you keep an eye on the sheep we already found. I'm gonna keep lookin'."

***

By midday, Hank's shirt stuck to his skin. He'd found more sheep along the trail and drove them back to Cottonwood Creek. He removed his canteen from his saddle and took a swig. The tracks continued northward.

"Mr. Patterson!" one of the ranch hands said. "It looks like the herd went and split round here."

Hank surveyed the trail. "Oh, shoot," he said to himself as he followed one fork in the tracks. He spurred his horse to a gallop when he saw the new set of tracks led toward a cliff. He felt his heart beating.

Hank slowed his horse near the cliff edge. He peered over. White splotches dotted the terrain below. He noticed some tracks leading off the cliff edge where the splotches were. His fist tightened. More bleating sounded in the distance behind him. He mopped his brow with his sleeve.

Following the trail away from the cliff, Hank discovered more sheep roaming the area. He breathed a sigh of relief as he determined they were the bulk of the flock.

***

It was late afternoon as Hank and his companions returned to the creek. The rest of the sheep continued to mill about. Aaron rode around them to keep the flock together with the other two ranch hands. Hank dismounted and splashed water on his face.

"You found them?" Aaron said as he walked his horse past his father.

"Mostly," Hank replied. "Looks like about a quarter of them got rimrocked. But the rest is okay. It's a miracle we found this many."

"Are we headin' back?"

"Sure. The rest of you go on home with the flock. I'm gonna head into Rockbed and see if the sheriff or Mr. Frazer knows anythin' 'bout what happened."

"Do you need any help, boss?" one of the ranch hands asked.

"No," Hank replied. "I ain't goin' to start a fight. I just want to talk. It'll likely be dark when I'm finished, so I won't be back until mornin'."

"Okay." The ranch hand nodded. "Good luck."

***

The sun set as Hank trotted into Rockbed. The sound of piano music and chatter emanated from the saloon. He hitched his horse and dismounted. A drunk ranch hand staggered out of the saloon and spat on the ground near Hank's feet. Hank stared at him.

"Your mother was good tonight," the man slurred.

Hank didn't answer. The man lumbered away. Hank patted his horse's mane and stepped inside.

They packed the saloon with trail hands at every table. Boisterous singing filled the room, but it fell silent as Hank entered. They turned and stared at him as he surveyed the room.

A white-bearded man sat in the corner with his back to the wall. "What are you doing here, Hank?" He stood up. "This is my night in the saloon. You ain't welcome here tonight."

"Good evenin' to you as well, Tom." Hank raised his hands. "I came here to talk."

"Well, I ain't available." Thomas Frazer sat down and folded his arms.

Hank walked toward Frazer's table. One man stuck his foot out and Hank fell forward as the patrons roared with laughter.

"Mind the step!" The patron guffawed.

Hank heaved himself to his feet and reached for his revolver. Chairs scraped. Some patrons ducked under the tables. Others pressed against the walls. Hank froze.

"Are you seriously gonna shoot me?" Frazer asked. "Don't worry, boys. He can't shoot all of us. Soon as he pulls the trigger, rush him."

Hank eased the gun out of the holster. He held it by the cylinder and handed it to the bartender. The ranch hands returned to their seats.

"I'll take a whiskey." Hank placed a nickel on the bar.

"You're lucky I don't allow firearms." The bartender uncorked a whiskey bottle. "Most of Frazer's boys want to shoot you."

"The feelin' is gonna be mutual." Hank took the filled glass. "His boys went and drove my flock off the pasture. Drove a couple of them off a cliff."

"So did you." Frazer walked over to the bar. "But at least I didn't kill nobody while doin' it."

Hank stopped before the whiskey touched his lips.

"You didn't know?" Frazer continued. "They shot one of my boys dead while tendin' to the flock. Your boys wouldn't have anythin' to do with that, would they?"

"My boys didn't do that." Hank downed the whiskey in one gulp.

"Then who did?" Frazer grabbed his shoulder. "That ain't cattle country, so Milt Boon ain't gonna be responsible. He's got nothin' to gain. There ain't nobody else with a spread nearby, so that kinda narrows it down."

Hank turned to face Frazer. He put his fists up. Frazer did the same. They circled. Two ranch hands grabbed Hank.

"Hey, take it outside!" the bartender said.

"He's all yours, boss!" one said.

"Let him go," Frazer replied. "Everyone step aside. We'll settle this out back like gentlemen."

"Fine." Hank wrenched his arms free. He followed Frazer to the yard behind the saloon, which was occupied by the outhouse and a trash heap, along with a wood pile. The smell made both men gag.

Frazer picked up a log and placed it on the ground between them.

Hank spat over it. "Let's begin." He took a swing at Frazer, who ducked.

"Kick his arse!" a ranch hand jeered.

Frazer jabbed Hank in the face twice. Hank screwed up his face. He charged forward. They both tumbled into the refuse pile. The spectators laughed. Hank choked. He stood up, pulling Frazer with him. He delivered a haymaker. Frazer went back into the trash pile. The spectators fell silent.

"Anyone else?" Hank looked around.

The ranch hands stepped back.

"I ain't done yet!" Frazer stood and tackled Hank.

His ranch hands cheered again.

The two men continued to wrestle. They made their way back inside the saloon. Frazer wrenched free of Hank's grip. He followed through with an uppercut. Hank flew back onto a table. His weight against the edge of the tabletop flipped it up. Bottles and glasses went flying. He groaned as more cheers arose.

"Life for a life, you murderin' bastard!" Frazer grabbed a broken bottle and stood over Hank.

Hank grabbed his wrist. The jagged tip of the glass almost touched his skin.

"That's enough!" A shot rang out.

Frazer loosened his grip on the bottle. Hank exhaled. Willie Snow entered the saloon gripping his smoking pistol.

"Glad you arrived, Sheriff," the bartender said. "Things were getting ugly between these feuding farmers."

"Everyone out." Snow gestured at the gathered ranch hands. "Which outfit are y'all with?"

"We all work for Mr. Frazer," one of the ranch hands said. "Mr. Patterson came here and started up a ruckus."

"Then Mr. Patterson can spend a night in the hoosegow." Snow holstered his gun.

Two of the ranch hands grabbed Hank and hauled him to his feet.

"Much obliged, Sheriff," Frazer said. "He's gotta pay for what he did."

Hank watched Frazer walk toward the door. His eyes narrowed.

"Where do you think you're going?" Snow grabbed Frazer's shoulder. "You're both under arrest."

The bar fell silent.

One laughed. "We're all Frazer's hands," he said. "You seriously think we're gonna let you take him in?"

"Don't be a fool," Frazer replied. "I'm going with them in order to clear this up. The rest of you can go home, unless our sheriff has any objection to that?"

Snow shook his head. "Only if they give me somethin' to object to."

***

Hank exchanged angry glances with Frazer as Snow escorted them down the street to the sheriff's office. They entered and made their way to the cells.

"Get inside." Snow opened the door to one cell.

Hank shoved Frazer inside. Frazer clenched his fists. The sound of a revolver being cocked prompted him to halt.

"If you don't stop fighting,"—Snow glowered at the pair of them—"I'm just gonna shoot you both."

Frazer stepped back. Hank slammed the cell door.

"Back." Snow gestured with the gun.

Hank obeyed. Snow stepped forward and locked Frazer's cell. He opened the cell opposite and gestured for Hank to enter. Hank stepped inside, listening to the metallic thud of the door being slammed behind him, followed by the rattle of keys in the lock.

Hank lay down on the rough wooden cot in the cell. The bumpiness of the surface against his back made him wince.

He heard a scraping sound outside, like a chair being dragged along the floor. He peered through the bars. Snow had brought the chair from his desk into the corridor between the two cells.

He sat down with a pipe in his hand. "While you're both sleepin' it off here…" He struck a match against the chair. "Maybe you can tell me what's happenin' between you. I'll start with Mr. Patterson. What was your business goin' to the saloon?"

"My flock had been driven off the communal pasture this mornin'." Hank breathed in the faint aroma of pipe smoke. "I figured Mr. Frazer had somethin' to do with it."

"Really?" Snow rolled his eyes and turned to Frazer. "And why would he do that?"

"Someone drove off my flock and killed one of my hired hands," Frazer replied. "I figured Mr. Patterson was somehow involved."

"You already came to me 'bout the shootin' of your hand." Snow blew out a cloud of smoke. "What makes you think Mr. Patterson was responsible for the killin'? Since you don't have no witnesses who can attest to him or any of his hands bein' present, you don't have a case."

"I don't need witnesses." Frazer spat a broken tooth through the bars. "Mr. Boon has offered that land to anybody for grazin' sheep since it ain't fit for steer. But his boys started demandin' tolls to drive our flocks to his land."

"And that ain't illegal." Snow wagged his finger. "The communal pasture is on Mr. Boon's spread, and he has a right to demand compensation from other outfits to pass through his land with their livestock."

"But why has he waited 'til now to charge us?" Frazer pressed against the bars. "He's never demanded money for passin' through before."

Hank rolled his eyes and lay back on the cot.

"That ain't none of my business," Snow said. "Your feud is causin' me no end of trouble. Mr. Boon wanted to facilitate all sheep farmers, but it seems like this place ain't big enough for the both of you."

"So he wants one of us out?" Frazer's voice cracked.

"If it keeps the peace," Snow replied. "What do you say, Mr. Patterson?"

"Maybe it's better if one of us left," Hank shouted through the bars. "I'm sure Milt will buy the land."

"Well, you can sleep on it," Snow replied. "I'll speak to Mr. Boon and see if he'll mediate a deal between you. But for now, keep your boys in check."

Chapter 12
Married to the Job

The sound of a door opening roused Carsten from his sleep. His face ached from where it had been resting on the desk. He sat up, trying to discern who had entered the office from his blurred vision.

"Working late?" a woman's voice said in a tone that carried both ridicule and concern.

Carsten rubbed his eyes as he saw Fleur standing in the doorway. "I'm sorry darlin'. I must have dozed off while writin' up the reports."

"Can't you delegate?" Fleur walked behind Carsten and massaged his shoulders. "Who normally deals with that?"

"Gibson," Carsten replied. "Besides, we ran into some trouble on the way to Yuma."

"Yes, I heard. Haven't you found somebody to take Gibson's place?"

"Still lookin'." Carsten rested his hand on Fleur's. He yawned.

"Here, I'll make some coffee." Fleur walked over to the stove.

Carsten smiled and nodded. "You know what? Why don't we head out to a café and get some breakfast? I reckon we both need some loafin' time."

The door to the office opened again. Wilkins stepped inside. "Howdy, Mrs. McNeil." He tipped his hat to Fleur. "Fell asleep at your desk, Marshal?"

"That's what it looks like," Carsten said. "I'm headin' out to breakfast with Fleur. Can you keep on things while I'm gone?"

"Sure thing," Wilkins replied. "What if the judge shows up?"

"Tell him I'm sick or something," Fleur said. "You could even tell him I'm pregnant. That'll hopefully get him to lay off for a while."

Carsten's eyes widened. She winked at him. He exhaled. She took his arm and led him outside. He shielded his eyes as he stepped from the gloomy office into the sunshine.

"I'm sure he'll be around to congratulate you," Wilkins said from inside the office.

"I'm sure he will." Fleur smiled to Carsten. "Come on, cowboy, let's go. No peace-keeping for you today."

***

The smell of freshly brewed coffee and the sound of conversation helped Carsten out of his stupor after they stepped into McCoy's Café. He removed his hat and surveyed the room. Phoenix's shop owners occupied the tables, dressed in jackets and Kentucky ties. They sat and dined with their wives or business partners. The occasional trail hand or teamster broke up the formal look of the clientele.

Arthur McCoy, a gray-bearded man in an apron, smiled at the couple. "Mornin', Marshal. Nice to see you again."

"Thanks, Arthur." Carsten nodded. "Just got back from Yuma only yesterday."

"Sounds like a busy trip." Arthur directed them to a vacant table. "Breakfast for two?"

"Much obliged," Carsten replied. "But call me Carsten. I'm off duty." He held out a chair for Fleur. She sat down. He sat opposite, placing his hat beneath his seat.

Arthur approached the table with a pot of coffee and two ceramic cups. Carsten watched steam dance around his cup as he poured the hot liquid in. He smiled at the café's owner.

"Late night?" Arthur said.

Carsten nodded.

"We've got a fresh batch of biscuits and gravy cooking," Arthur said. "That ought to wake you up if the coffee doesn't."

"That sounds wonderful," Fleur replied.

"Coming right up," Arthur said.

Carsten watched him return to the counter.

"Penny for your thoughts?" Fleur took a sip of coffee. "Let me guess, it's involving either Gibson or that fella who eluded you."

"I guess it's both." He took a long drink from his coffee. "How's Rowena holdin' up?"

"She's been withdrawn for a while, but she joined the ladies' circle again."

"That's good." Carsten smiled.

"Carsten, don't think about the job today." Fleur leaned closer. "You married me, not the Marshal Service. Bigamy's a crime. And you don't want to arrest yourself."

"I guess not." He chuckled. "All right, I'll take the day off today. Wilkins and Brennan should keep things in check. Maybe after breakfast we can take a walk."

"I'd like that." Fleur smiled. "It's been a while since we had a day where we spent time together, just the two of us."

"Yeah, I'm sorry about that. I guess I've been out and about so much."

Fleur gave a curt nod. Carsten fidgeted as he met her glare. A faint smile came to her lips.

Arthur returned to their table with their food. Carsten nodded a thanks. He breathed in the smell of the meat and black pepper. The two ate in silence. Carsten gave an approving nod as he tasted bits of bacon in the gravy.

After a bit, Arthur returned to collect the empty plates.

"Delicious, as always," Carsten said. "How much do we owe you?"

"That'll be one dollar," Arthur replied.

Carsten fished a dollar bill from his pocket and handed it over.

"You doin' much else today?" Arthur stuffed the bill into his apron pocket.

"Figured Fleur and me would go for a walk." Carsten scooped his hat from beneath his chair. "I'm gonna have to head out again real soon, but we both reckon I need to get some quality time with my wife before then."

"That sounds great," Arthur said. "You both have a good day now."

Carsten tipped his hat and left the café with Fleur.

The couple stepped outside. Carsten pulled his hat low to shield his eyes from the late morning sun.

"Where do you want to go?" Fleur asked.

"It's up to you. Shall we walk along the canal?"

"That sounds nice." Fleur smiled.

Carsten nodded in agreement. He extended his arm, and she took it. The couple walked down the street. He tipped his hat to passersby and exchanged nods with passing riders.

"Marshal McNeil?" Orville Gilbert waved at him from across the street.

"Always something…" Carsten muttered to Fleur.

"Do you have a minute?" The reporter jogged across the street.

A lumber wagon rolled along, almost hitting him. "Get outta the way, you tinhorn!" the driver shouted.

Orville wiped sweat from his brow and brushed trail dust from his jacket.

"What do you want to talk about, other than how to safely cross the street?" Carsten said.

"I was wondering if you had a comment on the attempted robbery on the Yuma train." Orville rummaged in his pockets for a notebook and pencil.

Fleur tightened her grip on Carsten's hand.

"No comment," Carsten replied. "I'm off duty, Mr. Gilbert. I'm sure my deputies can give their own accounts of what happened back at the office."

Fleur smiled and nodded in agreement.

"If'n you wish to talk to me 'bout it," Carsten said, "I'll be at my office in the mornin'."

Orville's mouth opened, but no sound came out. He looked between Carsten and Fleur. They both stared him down. He loosened his tie.

"I'll speak to you then." He snapped the notebook shut and pocketed it. "Ma'am." He tipped his hat to Fleur and walked away.

"Somethin' tells me we're gonna get a lot of that..." Carsten said.

"Well, at least Mr. Gilbert had the sense to back down." Fleur smiled. "You never were keen on talking to reporters, were you?"

"Nope. I never enjoyed gettin' publicity for the things I do. Anyhow, I don't think I should talk 'bout work today, like you said at breakfast."

"I agree. Let's just enjoy the day while we still have it to ourselves."

***

By the early afternoon, Carsten and Fleur sat by the canal on Van Buran Street. They pressed their backs against one of the nearby trees, taking advantage of the shade it offered. He watched as river barges moored nearby, so their crews could hunker down beneath their cargo to nap.

"This reminds me of that picnic by Lynx Lake," Fleur said.

"Our first outing together." Carsten waved his hat to fan them both. "Unless you count that time we saved Attie."

"That wasn't exactly the two of us." Fleur laughed. "Little crowded back then. With your brother Morris, Davey and Mike, and Benny. I miss them."

"I do too. I ought to write them a letter. I guess I've just been so busy. Didn't Attie and Davey have their first child last year? Maybe it's time we did a thing like that. I ain't plannin' on bein' a lawman for the rest of my days. You know that, don't you?"

"Yes." Fleur stared into the distance.

"I know." Carsten placed his arm over her shoulder. "The canal here ain't as nice as Lynx Lake back home. But we'll be returnin' there soon enough."

Fleur rested her head on Carsten's shoulder. "Who will you be going after next?"

"I believe his handle's Todd Moony. Wanted for murder. I'm headin' out to Globe tomorrow. But we don't have to talk 'bout that now." He looked toward one barge.

A crowd had gathered, staring at something he couldn't see. One fair-haired man, no older than twenty, had a gun drawn and pointed toward the barge.

"What's happenin' over there?" he said.

"I'm gonna kill you, you son of a bitch!" someone on the barge yelled.

"Fleur, stay here." Carsten stood up and drew his Remington. "If'n whatever happens escalates, we'll both get caught up in it."

Two men grappled with each other on the deck as he approached the barge. Carsten glimpsed the sun reflecting off blades in both their hands.

"What's goin' on?" Carsten asked a bystander. A badge was on the man's vest. The man's hands were shaking, which caused the gun to rattle. The gun had an uncocked hammer.

"Maybe some kinda argument over a card game from last night," the deputy said. "Maybe somethin' said taken as insultin' or maybe it's the heat. I'm kinda stumped. I've been told this ain't the first time these boys have tussled."

"Put the gun away, sonny." Carsten holstered his own revolver. "You ain't gonna need it for a thing like that."

"Carsten McNeil, what are you doing?" Fleur marched up to him. "Let this lawman handle it."

"Stay behind me." He gestured for her to halt. "You ain't armed, and this could get ugly."

The two fighters on the boat stopped at the mention of his name.

The man on the ground stared at him. "Carsten McNeil?"

The second man stood up and backed away.

"So, you know me?" Carsten folded his arms. "That'll save time on explainin'. What's this fracas about? What's the beef between the two of you that needs them Arkansas toothpicks you're carryin'?"

The two men looked at each other and shrugged.

"Zeke said some real unkind things 'bout my sister, who's in bed with the black lung," one of them said.

"I didn't mean to say anythin' among them lines," Zeke replied. "I simply asked Dick here if Verd was still bedridden. He must've misheard it."

"Well, it ain't worth dyin' over." Carsten's eyes narrowed. "So it ain't worth my time. Is it?"

The fighters shook their heads.

"I ain't got no beef with you," Dick said. "I don't want no trouble with the law."

"Then you'd best get gone," Carsten said.

Dick nodded in agreement. He sheathed his knife and walked away. Zeke nodded and sat back against a crate on the barge.

"It's okay, folks." Carsten surveyed the onlookers. "You can go 'bout your business. Maybe when it ain't as hot, those two folks can bury the hatchet."

The crowd dispersed. The man with the badge stood and stammered.

"What seems to be the trouble, deputy?" Carsten patted him on the shoulder.

"I'm sorry," the man said. "It's my first day sworn in, and I'm makin' my rounds. I'm Clifford Duncan, deputy marshal."

"Carsten McNeil." Carsten shook his hand. "I'm the US Marshal for the Arizona Territory. This here's my wife, Fleur."

"Ma'am." Clifford tipped his hat to Fleur.

"You must be Gibson's replacement," Carsten said. "Did Wilkins send you out here?"

Clifford nodded.

"Well, you got a lot to learn," Carsten said. "Havin' that badge don't mean a thing if you're dealin' with folks who don't respect it. And that hog leg ain't gonna be much use if you don't know how to use it."

"What do you mean?" Clifford scratched his head.

"You didn't cock it," Carsten said. "If it ain't cocked, it don't shoot. If those boys took offense to you steppin' in, you'd have been stuck like a hog. Now, head back to the office. We'll see if'n you can make a decent clerk if nothin' else."

"Right, marshal." Clifford tipped his hat. "Oh, I forgot. The judge wants to speak to you. He said he'd visit your office later on."

"You go on ahead." Carsten waved the young deputy away. "I'll be right there." Carsten turned to Fleur. "I'm sorry. I know I promised I wouldn't be workin' today."

"It's fine," she replied with a curt tone. "You're married to your job, after all."

"Fleur, please. Let's just enjoy the day."

"There are probably still crimes to fight." Tears welled in Fleur's eyes. "I don't want to get in the way of that. Besides, I need to visit Rowena."

"We can go together…" Carsten extended his hand.

She brushed it away and left.

He sighed and sat back down against the tree.

***

Later in the afternoon, Carsten returned to his office. Clifford sat at the desk, cleaning three revolvers. The gun's components cluttered the desk. Wilkins and Moses sat nearby, sipping coffee.

"What do you think of the tenderfoot, Marshal?" Wilkins asked.

"I see you got him to clean your guns," Carsten said, not making eye contact.

"Well, you know how it is with the empty sleeve," Wilkins said. "Did you have a nice day out with Mrs. McNeil?"

Carsten glowered at his deputy. Wilkins fidgeted. He and Moses stepped outside.

"I'm sorry, Marshal." Clifford stood up and made to follow them.

"You're fine," Carsten said. "Keep the desk. Maintaining Deputy Wilkins's guns is a regular task that everyone takes turns doin'. But if I was you, I'd get it finished 'fore the judge gets here. He chews out folks for messy desks."

"Right." Clifford sat down. "I don't mean to pry, but is your wife upset at you?"

"I ain't lookin' to talk 'bout that right now," Carsten snarled.

"Course not." Clifford raised his hands. "I was just concerned that I might have been a cause of something bad between you."

"That ain't your fault," Carsten said with a sigh. "I could have walked away, and I didn't. Fleur really wanted to be a deputy marshal. We've been through some tough scrapes before. But the judge wouldn't have none of it. He was gonna charge me with contempt of court if I tried anythin'. Things have been real tense at home ever since. Plus, she's gettin' homesick. Most of our friends and family live closer to Prescott than Phoenix."

Clifford fell silent.

"You want some coffee?" Carsten walked over to the stove.

"I'm good, thanks." Clifford reassembled one pistol.

"What were you doin' before you got sworn in?" Carsten put a heaped spoon of ground coffee into the pot. "I normally hand-pick most of my deputies."

"Well, I got appointed by the judge." Clifford fidgeted. "I was workin' at the federal court as a filin' clerk and wanted to try out bein' a lawman."

The door to the office opened. Judge Stanley stepped inside. "Good afternoon, Marshal McNeil." He removed his hat. "I'm glad you could make it today."

"I'm sorry for the mess, your honor," Carsten replied. "My new deputy only told me 'bout this meetin' today."

"That's what I came to talk to you about," the judge said. "Marshal McNeil, this here's my nephew, Clifford Duncan. I swore him in as a US Deputy Marshal this morning."

Carsten gulped. "Yes. We met earlier today. I saw him tryin' to intervene in a fight by the canal."

"What were you doing by the canal?" Stanley asked after a brief pause.

"Goin' for a walk with Fleur, your honor," Carsten said. "Since I was in town, I figured we'd spend the day together. I'm headin' out to Globe tomorrow to find the wanted killer Todd Moony."

"That's good to know," the judge said. "Because you can take Clifford with you. Teach him the ropes. I know you'll be stepping down soon. You've assembled a fine body of deputies."

"Which I normally hand-pick, your honor." Carsten forced a smile. "I don't want to be responsible for watchin' over your kin 'fore he's seen the elephant."

"I understand your concern," the judge said. "But this assignment comes with a bonus." He reached into his pocket and produced another marshal badge.

"You mean, I get to appoint another deputy?" Carsten asked. "Like who?"

"I heard about the incident at the canal." Stanley threw his arm over Carsten's shoulder. "Clifford went by the courthouse after you sent him here. Plus I talked with your deputies outside. I can't have my best lawman's troubles at home affecting the work he does."

"You mean...?" Carsten stammered.

"That's right." The judge grinned. "You take on my nephew, and I'll let you take on your wife as a deputy. Now, find Todd Moony and bring him to justice. Do we have a deal?"

"We have a deal, your honor." Carsten shook his hand.

"Don't let me down." Judge Stanley put on his hat and left.

***

Carsten admired the stars in the cloudless night as he walked back home. He stopped for a moment as he arrived on the porch. He removed his boots and fished the deputy's badge out of his pocket.

"Honey, I'm home!" He stepped through the door to no response. The kitchen was empty. Two suitcases sat by the door. He lifted one of them, feeling the weight. Carsten knocked on the door of the bedroom. He leaned against the wood and heard weeping from inside. He opened the door. Shadows bathed the room except where the light from the hallway shone inside. Fleur sat on the bed and faced the wall. She buried her head in her hands as she wept.

"Fleur?" Carsten said with a soft tone. "Can I sit with you a spell?"

"Sure," she said through her tears.

Carsten sat on the bed next to her. He placed his arm over her shoulder. "I'm sorry 'bout today."

"You keep saying that. But it never changes. I love watching you work, but I hate not being able to work with you. You're never around because you're always on the trail of some outlaw. And even when you are in town, you're always busy. So I've decided to go back to Cripple Gorge. I'm packing my bags and leaving on the morning train. You can either leave with me, or you can stay here if you care more about your duty."

"You can leave if you wish. But I wanted to tell you somethin' that happened today. After that meetin' I had with the judge, we're headin' out to Globe tomorrow."

"We?" Fleur said. "You're still choosin' to ride out with your deputies?"

"I said we, not I." He handed his wife the deputy marshal's badge. "But I'm takin' on some new deputies."

"What's this?" Fleur asked.

"You could still say I'm ridin' out with my deputies tomorrow. So I'm offerin' another option. You can ride to Globe with me and catch this fella we're huntin'."

"Really?" Fleur wiped the tears from her eyes. "What about Judge Stanley? You said he was goin' to charge you if you tried to deputize me."

"He gave me that badge." Carsten grinned. "That new deputy we saw turned out to be his nephew. I said I'd take him on if'n I could take you on as well. Just like old times?"

"Just like old times." She smiled. "Who are we goin' after?"

"Todd Moony. Wanted for murder."

"Doesn't sound any different from most of the folks we've fought." Fleur stood up and walked out of the bedroom. She returned a moment later with a lamp from the kitchen.

Carsten struck a match and lit the lamps on the wall. Their dim glow chased away the shadows in the room.

Fleur opened a dresser drawer. She produced the Webley Bulldog she kept there.

"Good choice," Carsten said. "But if you're a deputy, I reckon you're gonna need somethin' bigger to wear on your hip."

"Don't you have that Colt for long-range shooting?"

"That could work."

"I think a couple of your older shirts and pants will fit me if I roll them in. Will we have time in the morning to stock up?"

"I reckon so." Carsten smiled. "It's at least three days' ride to Globe from Phoenix. But I can delay things while we pick up some suitable ridin' attire and a bigger gun. But for now, you see what you'll be comfortable ridin' in. I'll rustle up some grub."

"We have got little in. But I can give you a hand if you wish."

He nodded and walked out of the bedroom.

"Carsten?" she said behind him.

"Yes, darlin'?" He looked back at her.

"Thank you."

Carsten stepped into the kitchen and opened the cupboards. He looked through various tins and bags of dried foodstuffs, including kidney beans and rice. Then he lit the stove.

As he turned around, Fleur emerged from the bedroom. She had exchanged her dress for a light blue shirt and trousers. "How do I look?" She leaned against the wall with her thumbs in her pockets.

"Almost ready to ride the range." He smiled. "Reckon we'll need to pick up some decent boots and a hat. Along with a horse."

She nodded. "Here's to working together again."

Chapter 13
On Todd Moony's Trail

A week later, Carsten led his deputies into Rockbed. The late afternoon sun bore down on them and sweat streamed down Carsten's face like tears. He looked around at the sleepy-looking frontier town. A few townspeople wandered the streets. They retreated into their homes upon seeing the posse approach.

"Place seems kinda dead," Wilkins commented.

"Not too different from Cripple Gorge," Fleur replied. She wore a pair of dark chaps and a wide-brimmed hat. A Colt Peacemaker sat in a holster on her hip.

"I don't blame them," Carsten said. "A large group of riders probably foretells trouble, badge or no badge. Especially with the sheriff in Globe sayin' Todd Moony was last seen headin' this way. He might have killed again."

A rotund man with a full beard stepped out of the sheriff's office. He carried a shotgun, which he had pointed at the ground. "What are you folks doin' in my town? You'd best state your business."

Carsten dismounted his horse. He walked up to the sheriff. "I'm US Marshal Carsten McNeil." He pulled back the lapel of his duster to reveal his marshal's badge. "We're lookin' for a dangerous outlaw believed to have passed through here."

"I'm Willie Snow." The sheriff propped the shotgun against the wall. "I'm the sheriff here. Do you have any description of the fella you're lookin' for?"

"Clifford, do you have the handbills?" Carsten turned to his new deputy.

Clifford took a drink from his canteen, dribbling some water. He rummaged through his saddlebags and produced a folded handbill. "Todd Moony," he read aloud in a hoarse voice. "Wanted for murder. We believed he'd gone to ground in Globe, but we picked up rumors he'd been sighted in Rockbed."

Carsten took the handbill from him. He showed the picture to the sheriff, who paused and looked at it.

"I ain't seen any fella lookin' like that." He shook his head.

"You sure?" Carsten stared at him. "That took some thinkin'."

"It's hot." Snow shrugged. "I don't think quickly when it's hot, and it's always hot 'round here."

"Well, we're gonna water our horses at the livery and then head into the saloon to get some vittles." Carsten tipped his hat. "If'n you can remember somethin', that's where you'll find us."

"Right." Snow walked back into the office.

Carsten nodded to his deputies. They hitched their horses and dismounted.

"How you feelin', Clifford?" Carsten gave him a friendly thump on the back.

"Beat," the young deputy croaked. "Never ridden at a pace like that before."

"Well, I'm glad you kept up without passin' out," Wilkins said with a grin.

Moses and Fleur laughed. Even Nastas cracked a smile.

"You've done great so far." Carsten grinned. "Come on, let's go. We can get somethin' to knock the trail dust out of our gullets and get some decent vittles."

After leaving the horses at the livery, Carsten led his posse into Rockbed's saloon. Empty tables filled the room, save for one occupied by three old-timers playing poker.

"It ain't often we get a posse comin' through here," one of them said.

Carsten tipped his hat to them.

"I know that fella," another said. "He looks like Carsten McNeil."

"I've heard of him," the third man said. "If he's comin' here, there might be some trouble loomin'."

A scrape of chairs followed. The three men stood up and left the saloon.

Carsten walked over to the bar. He noticed the bartender's hands shaking.

"What'll it be, strangers?" he stammered.

"We'll have beers all around," Carsten said. "Do you serve food here?"

"Just beans," the bartender said. "Maybe with bacon."

"Anythin' will do." Carsten scattered coins on the counter. "We've been ridin' from Phoenix. And get yourself some whiskey. You're lookin' a mite fearful with no real need to be."

The bartender nodded.

"Place seems pretty dead." Carsten looked around. "Somethin' happened in this town recently?"

"Range war." The bartender spilled whiskey on the bar. He took the filled glass and downed it in one gulp. "The Pattersons and the Frazers have been at each other's throats for the past month."

"Who are they?" Carsten asked.

"Sheep farmers," the bartender said. "I try to let different outfits drink here on different days, otherwise they start brawlin', and my place gets smashed up. Willie Snow's got his work cut out for him right now, and Mr. Boon is tryin' to mediate things. Not the kinda thing you'd expect from a cattleman."

Carsten exchanged a glance with his deputies. "That's interestin'." He leaned closer. "Can you tell me anymore?"

"Not right now." A bead of sweat ran down the bartender's cheek. "That's all I've really seen."

"Well, thanks for sharin', but that ain't why I'm here." Carsten laid out Todd Moony's handbill on the countertop. "I'm lookin' for this fella. Have you seen him?"

"I know that fella." The bartender studied the drawing on the poster. "He was in here a couple of weeks ago. Some stranger came in and got into a punch-up with some of Mr. Patterson's boys. Then the sheriff came in and arrested him for stealin' a horse from one of Mr. Boon's hands. The fella in the poster was with the sheriff."

"What did the fella who stole the horse look like?" Carsten gestured for Clifford to join him.

"Long hair and a moustache," the bartender said. "Looked like a saddle tramp. Hadn't seen him before, neither."

"Clifford, do you have the handbill for Blaine Weber?" Carsten asked.

Clifford unfolded the sheet and showed it to the bartender.

"That's the fella." He nodded. "Sheriff took him in with that Moony fella."

"So he's in jail?" Carsten asked.

"If he stole a horse, he's probably buried somewhere on the prairie," the bartender said. "I'm sorry, Marshal. I have little more for you than that."

"You've been helpful enough already," Carsten replied. "My deputies and me are gonna get our beers and find a couple of tables while it's still quiet."

"Of course." The bartender nodded. "And I have some workin' girls if you're lookin' for some company."

Carsten shook his head. He raised his hand to show the ring on his finger. He glanced aside, seeing Fleur give him a proud smile.

***

Four trail hands entered the saloon, along with some local shopkeepers. Carsten sat at a table in the saloon's corner with Fleur and Clifford. He sat with his back to the wall and watched the room fill. A half-empty glass of beer sat beside the remains of a plate of pork and beans. Wilkins, Moses, and Nastas sat together in the opposite corner of the saloon.

"I don't know 'bout you," Carsten said, "but this town is startin' to get more interestin' than I initially figured it would."

"Do you reckon there'll be trouble while we're here?" Fleur asked.

"I reckon that's a given in any saloon." Carsten turned to Clifford. "If'n things get heated, don't start shootin' unless they shoot first. If a punch-up starts, use the butt of your iron and hit 'em over the head. That'll put most folks out of action."

"You reckon?" Clifford asked.

"It works for me." Carsten leaned back in his chair. "Nothin' hurts like gettin' pistol-whipped. Gettin' shot or stabbed can be permanent, but that ain't the case with a pistol-whippin'."

"I'll have to bear that in mind," Clifford said.

"Please do." Carsten nodded. "Now, I reckon if'n some punches do start flyin', then the sheriff will come and intervene. I wanna see what happens. Can you handle that?"

"There's somethin' that's been gnawin' at me since we sat down." Clifford fidgeted.

"Well, if the cat's outta the bag, it's a sight easier to let 'em out than put 'em back in." Carsten patted him on the arm. "At least, that's what my pa says. What's on your mind?"

"The bartender was talkin' 'bout brawls between the Patterson and Frazer outfits." Clifford put his hands together. "But he didn't say anythin' of the sort 'bout that cattleman's outfit. Do you reckon they're gonna fit in this somewhere?"

"Yeah, I thought that as well," Fleur said.

Carsten nodded. He watched two more men in trail clothes enter the saloon. The patrons at the tables stared at them. "Well," he said, "I reckon we're about to find out."

The two newcomers approached the bar and handed over their guns. They exchanged glances with Carsten's deputies while keeping their distance. They exchanged harder stares with the trail hands at the tables.

"What's the plan, Marshal?" Clifford whispered.

"We wait," Carsten said. "See what happens. If'n there's a brawl, let them duke it out for a spell and see if somebody gets the sheriff. I want to see whose side he's takin'. If it gets ugly, we step in."

"Right," Clifford said.

The two men leaned on the bar and sipped glasses of beer.

"Hey!" One of the trail hands at the table stood up. "What are Frazer's boys doin' here? It's our night tonight."

"Those must be Patterson's men." Carsten gestured for the deputies at the other table to remain seated.

The Frazer hands remained at the bar, not making eye contact.

"Hey, I'm talkin' to you!" the Patterson hand shouted.

Chairs scraped. The other three Patterson hands stood up. A shopkeeper ran out of the saloon.

"I'd guess he's goin' to the sheriff," Clifford said.

The four Patterson hands strode over to the two Frazer hands. The bartender ducked.

"It's Patterson night tonight," the burliest hand said. "Frazer boys ain't welcome here on Patterson nights."

He yanked the Frazer hand's shoulder, who threw the contents of his glass into the bully's face. Another Patterson hand took a swing at him. The other two grabbed the second Frazer man's arms, then punched him in the stomach. The first Frazer man lay on the floor. The two Patterson men kneeled over and punched him.

"Let's go. Follow my lead." Carsten stood up. He strode over to the bar. "That's enough!"

"This ain't your business, sonny." One of the Patterson hands looked up. "Back off if you want to keep that pretty face of yours."

"I ain't askin' again." Carsten eased his Colt Frontier out of its holster. He gripped it by the barrel. "Get off them. Shindig's over."

The bully clenched his fist. He stood up. Carsten swung the Colt into his face. The bully fell back.

"Son of a whore!" The Patterson hand clutched his face, blood seeping through his fingers.

Moses stepped forward with his shotgun. He clubbed another Patterson hand in the back. He fell to the floor. A third grabbed a bottle and faced Carsten. A click stopped him. Fleur aimed her Peacemaker at him and shook her head. More clicks followed. Nastas, Moses, and Wilkins aimed their guns at the other two Patterson hands. They stood against the bar and raised their hands.

"Y'all had better clear outta here before the sheriff arrives," Carsten said to the three hands. "Your spokesman there can stay right here. I got some questions for him. The Frazer boys as well. But we'll keep their hoglegs. They can collect them in the mornin'."

The two hands nodded. They hauled the second man to his feet and stepped outside.

"I think he broke my nose!" the bully screamed.

"That I did." Carsten holstered his gun. He walked over to the bully and extended his hand. "But you gave me no choice."

"I'd kill you if I had my gun." The bully knocked Carsten's hand away.

Willie Snow entered the saloon with his shotgun held at the ready. "What's goin' on here? You causin' trouble, Carsten?"

"Just doin' your job for you," Carsten said. "Keepin' the peace in this little burg."

"You'd best ride on." Snow advanced on Carsten. He thumbed back the hammers on his shotgun. "I already told you Todd Moony ain't here. Now you're stirrin' up trouble for the good townsfolk."

Nastas aimed his revolver at the sheriff's head. He froze.

"You have some explainin' to do, Sheriff." Carsten folded his arms. "You said Todd Moony ain't here, but I heard he helped you bring in a horse thief I've also been lookin' for."

"And who told you that?" Snow's eyes narrowed.

"That ain't important." Clifford stepped forward. "But what is important is what you done told us is an obstruction of justice."

"That's true." Carsten gave his deputy an approving nod. "You're under arrest, Sheriff. I'd lower that shotgun if I were you."

His other deputies trained their guns on the sheriff. He uncocked and lowered the shotgun.

"Deputy Brennan, would you disarm the sheriff?" Carsten said.

"Sure, Marshal." Moses handed his shotgun over to him. He lumbered over to Snow and snatched the shotgun away, along with the revolver in the sheriff's holster.

"Nastas," Carsten said, "you take this so-called lawman back to his jail. I'll talk to him later. Take Wilkins and Brennan with you."

The deputy nodded in response. He gestured with his gun. The sheriff walked out of the saloon, followed by the three deputies.

"Carsten McNeil?" The bully froze. "You're that lawman from the courthouse siege. I'm sorry. I didn't mean to threaten you."

"That's all right." Carsten offered his hand again. "And to make up for it, I'd like to buy you a drink. Those Frazer boys too. This place has gotten real interestin' real fast, and I'd like to know what's happenin'."

"Well, I ain't keen on jawin' 'bout the town with strangers." The Patterson man took Carsten's hand. "But I wouldn't say no to a drink."

"You suggestin' we drink with that curly wolf?" One of the Frazer hands spat a broken tooth onto the floor.

"As a matter of fact, I am." Carsten nodded as he helped him to his feet. He peered over the bar where the bartender hid. "I wanna know what's goin' on here, and I'd like to keep things cordial if you don't mind."

"Fine," the hand said.

"I'd like a bottle of whiskey and six glasses, if you're still open for business," Carsten said.

The bartender laid the bottle and glasses on a tray. Carsten noticed his hands trembling.

"Here." He placed two dollars on the counter. "Let me get that for you."

Fleur and Clifford helped the other Frazer hand to his feet. Carsten looked down for a moment as he saw their bruises. They walked back to Carsten's table. He uncorked the bottle of whiskey and poured each of them a glass.

"Your health, fellas." Carsten raised his glass.

The others raised their own.

"What do you want to know?" The Patterson hand sipped his whiskey.

"For a start, I'd like to know what your names are," Carsten said. He gestured to Clifford, who sat poised with a pencil and notebook.

"My name's Harvey," he said. "I'm a hired hand workin' for Hank Patterson."

"I'm Roy," the first Frazer hand said. "And my friend's Al. We both work for Thomas Frazer."

Al exchanged a nod with Carsten.

"Now, what's this here feud about?" Carsten asked.

"A friend of ours got killed while tending the flock on pasture," Roy said. "Good grazin' is gettin' scarce, but Mr. Boon has some suitable land on his spread. It ain't fit for cattle, so he offered it to the sheep farmers. But his boys started chargin' us to drive sheep through his lands. Said it was to compensate for the damage they cause."

"That don't make much sense," Clifford said. "Are sheep really that bad for the land?"

"When you got a couple mean-lookin' cowboys threatenin' to scatter your flock, there ain't much room to argue that." Harvey folded his arms.

"The bartender was sayin' you got into a range war," Carsten said.

"One of the Frazer hands apparently got shot tendin' the flock like those fellas said," Harvey replied. "And they started pointin' the finger at Mr. Patterson."

"Who else could it be?" Roy got up and loomed over Harvey.

"Y'all simmer down," Carsten said with a cutting tone, and Roy sat back. "Do you any of you ever encounter Mr. Boon's men in here?"

The three hands exchanged glances and shrugs with one another.

"His boys never really come to town," Roy said.

"Yeah." Harvey stroked his chin. "I heard he built a whorehouse on his own ranch. One that only serves his men."

Carsten's head tilted to the side. "Can you tell me anythin' else?" He leaned closer.

"Not really." Harvey shrugged. "Far as I'm concerned, that's just a rumor."

"In that case, we're done here," Carsten said. "But perhaps you can help me with one thing. Do any of you recognize this fella?" He produced Todd Moony's handbill.

"I saw him!" Al said. "We saw him with the sheriff a while back after gettin' into a fight with a horse thief. He was with Demon Eyes too."

"Demon Eyes?" Fleur's eyebrow rose.

"Norman Reid," Harvey said. "He's Mr. Boon's foreman, and he's bad news. I heard the man's a stone-cold killer. He's always scowlin', and it's like bein' stared down by the devil himself."

Al and Roy nodded in agreement.

"Did the other fella look like this?" Carsten showed Blaine Weber's handbill.

"That's the fella!" Al said. "We thought he was one of Patterson's hands, so we jumped him."

Roy nudged Al and hushed him.

"That don't matter," Carsten said. "Do you know where he went when the sheriff came?"

"I figured they took him to jail," Roy said. "But if Demon Eyes was with him, the other fella is probably workin' for Mr. Boon. If he stole a horse from Mr. Boon, he's probably dead now."

"Does Mr. Boon keep a spread 'round here?" Carsten asked.

"He does," Harvey said. "But it's more like a fort than a ranch. Adobe walls patrolled by men with rifles. Big heavy gate. Expectin' some kind of moat and drawbridge affair."

The other ranch hands laughed, which gave way to winces.

Carsten straightened his posture at the remark. "Like some kind of compound?"

"So I've heard." Harvey shrunk back. "I ain't been there myself, though. Just heard stories."

"I'm much obliged." Carsten stood up with Fleur and Clifford. "Harvey, since you were the one who started the fight, you're gettin' a choice: either pay these two fellas five dollars each in compensation, or you can spend a night in the hoosegow."

Al and Roy looked at him and grinned.

"I ain't got that kinda money on me." Harvey held his hands together, smirking in response to Al and Roy's pouts. "Looks like you gotta take me in."

Carsten handcuffed him.

"What about us?" Al said.

"You two go home," Carsten said. "If'n you're in a fit shape to do so."

"We've both been beaten into cocked hats worse than this," Roy said.

"You take care now," Carsten said. "This fella ain't gonna be botherin' you again."

"There is somethin'," Roy said. "When we got into the fight with that Blaine fella, I found a letter he'd dropped. I thought it was some love letter, but then I read it."

"And what was it?" Fleur stared at him.

"I don't have it with me, but it was from someone named Amy Filmore." Roy fidgeted. "Some kind of mail-order bride or something whose prospective husband sold her. Said she was bein' held in the compound."

"Did you report this to the sheriff?" Carsten asked.

"No." Roy shook his head. "The letter mentioned a brother in Boston, so I rode to Globe and sent a wire to him and called that my good deed for the day."

"Why didn't you tell the sheriff?" Fleur loomed over them.

Roy gestured for Carsten to come closer. "If this involves Mr. Boon," he whispered, "then the sheriff is the last person we ought to be speakin' to."

Carsten nodded in understanding.

"We can take statements from them," Clifford said. "That ought to be enough for a warrant."

"I think Al and I need to be gettin' some rest," Roy said. "We can give our statements in the morning."

The two hands staggered out of their chairs. They collected their guns from the bartender and left the saloon.

***

After locking Harvey in a cell, Carsten stood outside the sheriff's office. It was a cloudless night, and he looked up at the stars.

Fleur stood beside him. "You were right. This town is just too interesting not to stay in."

"There's somethin' else," Carsten replied. "When we took Bowman Ratcliff to Yuma, he talked 'bout bein' sheltered at some compound."

"What are you thinking?" She rested a hand on his shoulder.

"I reckon Mr. Boon has some explainin' to do. Maybe he's shelterin' desperadoes there. And he's involved in some kinda slavery ring."

"Don't we need some kind of proof? We don't have the letter, and we'll need Al and Roy to give a statement."

"We do. I reckon I ought to pay Mr. Boon a visit in the mornin'. Get things from his point of view if anythin'."

"Maybe the sheriff can help us. From what Al said, he's in Mr. Boon's pocket and might be inclined to share the details."

"Maybe you're right." Carsten turned around. "Let's ask him."

The couple entered the sheriff's office. Wilkins, Moses, and Clifford sat around the desk with a frayed pack of cards. Nastas sat away from them. He rested his Winchester on his lap and stared toward the cells.

"You care to join us, Marshal?" Clifford asked. "I offered a place to Nastas. I figured I might offer it to you and Fleur."

"I'm in," Fleur said. She pulled up a chair and sat down.

"I'll join you directly," Carsten replied. "First, I'd like to speak with our host." Carsten dragged another chair to the cells. He placed it in front of Willie Snow's cell and sat down. "You have some explainin' to do, Sheriff. Not only have you lied 'bout Todd Moony, but you might also be coverin' for somethin' bigger."

"Like what?" Snow lay back on the wooden cot and faced the wall.

"Does the name Amy Filmore mean anythin' to you?" Carsten said.

"Should it?" Snow replied.

"You've already got obstruction charges floatin' over you." Carsten stood up. "Do you want bribery in there as well? What does Mr. Boon want with Miss Filmore?"

"I don't know anythin' about Miss Filmore." Snow looked back at Carsten. "My job is to keep the peace in this town and make sure things don't get too heated between the Patterson and Frazer outfits. That's all."

"And you've been doin' a good job of that so far." Carsten rolled his eyes. "Tell me what you know, and I'll put in a good word with the judge for you."

"I ain't interested." Snow turned away again.

"What are you afraid of?"

"I'm dead if I tell you," Snow said. "Word of this will get back to Mr. Boon somehow. Now leave me alone. Go join your card game."

"Fine." Carsten's fist tightened. "But you need to think 'bout whether you want to open up 'bout all this." Carsten returned to the main office. He brought the chair back to the desk where his deputies continued to play cards. "Room for one more?"

"The night is young," Wilkins replied. He sat in a slouched position with his cards facedown. He lifted them. "I'm folding from this round."

"That sheriff seemed tight-lipped," Clifford said. "How do we convince him to talk?"

"For now, we do nothin'," Carsten replied. "It ain't right to beat on a fella to get info."

"You've never done that?" Clifford asked.

"Not when I was a lawman," Carsten said. "I did it once before when my sister got kidnapped. But the case might get dismissed if we try that now. Tomorrow, I'm gonna head over to Mr. Boon's ranch."

***

"Help! Sheriff! Come quick!" The shouting echoed through the streets.

Carsten forced his eyes open. He winced as the early morning sun shone through the shutters in his hotel room. He heaved himself out of bed.

"What's happening?" Fleur sat up next to him.

Carsten walked over to the window. He looked toward the sheriff's office across the street. Several bystanders, alerted to the shouting, stared at a haggard-looking rider. He dismounted outside the office. Clifford and Nastas emerged from within. They walked across the street toward the hotel.

"Looks like trouble." Carsten grabbed a bundle of clothes. "Best get some clothes on. We've got visitors."

After getting dressed, the couple walked downstairs into the hotel's foyer. They heard the sound of heavy panting as they approached. Clifford and Nastas waited by the front desk with a man in trail clothes.

"What's goin' on?" Carsten asked.

"This fella's Hutch Scanlon," Clifford said. "He's foreman for Thomas Frazer. Just came by the office and said they found two of his employees bushwhacked on the trail."

Carsten's eyes widened.

"That doesn't sound good," Fleur said. "Do you think it could have been…?"

"I reckon," Carsten said. "We'd better mount up. I'll get Wilkins and Moses to watch the jail."

"What happened to the sheriff?" Hutch asked.

"He's under arrest for obstruction of justice," Carsten replied. "I'm Carsten McNeil, US Marshal for the Arizona Territory. I'm here in pursuit of an outlaw and stumbled across this range war business."

"Well, I'd say it's about time." Hutch scratched his head.

"Come on." Carsten led him toward the door. "You can lead us to where they were found."

***

The heat bore down on the posse as they rode along the trail from Rockbed. Carsten yawned as he followed Hutch. He struggled to keep his eyes open as his horse trotted along.

"Marshal!" Clifford pointed toward the sky.

Carsten squinted ahead. He made out the shape of vultures circling in the distance. "That must be them." His heart pounded, and he felt awake. He spurred his horse into a lope.

The posse reached the area the vultures circled over two dead men by the trail. Carsten yanked his horse's reins to stop him. He dismounted and walked over to the first body. A trail of dried blood ran from the center of the dirt path toward the brush, stopping near the body. The dead man lay on his back, with a large gunshot wound in the chest and another in the head. Carsten held his hat to his chest as he recognized Al's face staring back at him. He waved at the flies that buzzed around, kneeled down, and closed his eyes.

"Are they the boys we spoke to last night?" Clifford said.

Carsten looked back and nodded. He turned to Roy's body, which lay a short distance from Al's. Another large gunshot wound in the torso. His head lay against a rock. He nodded to Nastas, who spurred his horse away.

"What do you mean you spoke to those boys last night?" Hutch said.

"We met them in the saloon after they got jumped by some of Patterson's hands." Carsten remounted his horse. "We intervened and detained the fella who started it, then we got to talkin' 'bout what happened here."

"Patterson..." Hutch spat on the ground. "I should have known."

"I ain't sure," Carsten said. "I sat with both Roy and Al, along with a Patterson fella named Harvey. They shared what they knew 'bout this valley, their feud, and a couple details 'bout Mr. Boon. I reckon someone didn't want certain things gettin' out."

Hutch raised an eyebrow but said nothing.

"What do you think happened, Marshal?" Clifford asked.

"Best guess," Carsten replied, "someone was usin' a Sharps from the hill. The holes in their chests look pretty big. Nastas used to be a scout for the army. He'll find out where they were firin' from."

"One of the other hired hands was killed with a Sharps too," Hutch said. "Fella was tendin' to the flock when someone shot him and drove our sheep away."

"Well this time you ain't gonna be pointin' the finger at Patterson," Carsten replied.

Nastas waved from a cluster of rocks by the hill.

"Looks like he found the hidin' spot," Carsten said.

The posse rode toward the hill while Nastas rode toward them.

"He's still followin' a trail," Carsten said. "But those rocks look like a good vantage point."

Nastas reached them. He held up one finger then kept moving.

"Only one person pulled off the bushwhack," Carsten said. "And it looks like they rode down here."

"They shot them from those rocks?" Fleur said.

"I reckon." Carsten put his hands together and closed his eyes. "They hit Al first. He went off his horse. But he was still breathin' when he hit the ground, so he tried to drag himself away. Roy probably turned and lit out. Then he got shot off his horse and hit his head against the rock. If the bullet didn't kill him, that would have. There was a full moon and no cloud last night, so our bushwhacker might have seen Al movin' and went to finish him off. That's why the tracks are comin' this way."

"I have a mind to go to the Patterson spread and get some payback." Hutch tightened his grip on his reins. "Mr. Frazer went and sold his land yesterday, so there ain't much here for me."

"You ain't gonna do nothin' of the kind." Carsten stared him down. "Hold on, you said he sold the land?"

Hutch nodded.

"Then Patterson ain't got much to gain from killin' anyone else of yours," Carsten said. "That's if he's got the land."

"He don't," Hutch said. "Frazer sold the land to Mr. Boon. I guess he wants to expand into sheep."

"Now that ain't somethin' that got brought up last night." Carsten's eyebrow rose.

"He announced it this mornin'," Hutch replied. "I was gonna ride into town to find Al and Roy when they didn't get back last night."

"What's the plan, Marshal?" Clifford asked.

"I want you and Fleur to pay a visit to the Patterson spread." Carsten pulled a piece of beef jerky from his pocket and chewed it. "Nastas and me are gonna try to pick up the shooter's trail. We'll catch the guy real soon. If it goes cold, we're gonna pay a visit to Mr. Boon."

Chapter 14
A Fulfilled Contract

Boon sat at his table on the porch and watched the late morning sunshine over his compound. He sipped a cup of coffee and leaned back in his chair.

Two riders approached the compound. He grabbed his walking stick and stood up to greet them. As they drew closer, he recognized them as Hank and Reid. "Mr. Patterson." He smiled. "I'm so glad you could accept my invitation. Care to join me for some coffee?"

Hank dismounted and followed Boon to the porch. Reid leaned on the wall nearby.

"When Mr. Reid comes by my place"—Hank sat down—"I figured I had little choice."

"Well, I'm still glad you came." Boon poured some coffee into a spare cup. "Today's a time to celebrate. Our mutual friend, Mr. Thomas Frazer, has sold us his land. The feud you both had is now ending."

"I suppose that's good news." Hank nodded as Boon slid the coffee cup over to him. "What does this do for our agreement? Will I be able to have that cattle you promised me?"

"Regrettably, circumstances have changed." Boon removed his hat and placed it to his chest. "It seems somebody else has gotten involved in your feud, and I'm concerned they may end up being tangled in my other business affairs."

"What does that mean?" Hank leaned closer.

"The saloonkeeper informed me that a posse of US Marshals arrived in Rockbed yesterday. They arrested my sheriff and intervened in a brawl between two sets of hired hands. If they believe you stood to gain from our arrangement, you may be in trouble."

"You mean… you're goin' back on our deal?" Hank stood up and loomed over Boon. "You promised me twenty head of cattle!"

"You had better calm down, or you'll cause a scene," Boon replied in a stern tone.

Reid stepped forward and rested his hand on his holster. Hank sat down. He trembled at Reid's harsh glare. The gunman folded his arms again. A man with a rifle approached the porch.

"What do you want?" Boon scowled at him. "I haven't finished my meeting with Mr. Patterson."

"Sorry, boss," the man replied. "It's just that there's a US Marshal McNeil at the gates. Said he wants to speak to you."

Reid's head snapped at the mention of the name.

"Fine, I'll speak to him." Boon stood up and picked up his walking stick. "Will you excuse me? Help yourself to more coffee." Boon followed the guard to the gates of the compound.

Two riders stood outside, near the guard shack. A brown-haired man in his mid-twenties with a youthful face was accompanied by a stern-looking Navajo man. Both men wore badges on their lapels.

"Good morning," Boon said. "I understand you wish to speak with me?"

"That depends," the first man replied. "Are you the owner of this spread?"

"That is correct." Boon doffed his hat. "My name is Milt Boon. How can I be of service?"

"I'm US Marshal Carsten McNeil. This here's my deputy, Nastas. We're on the trail of a gunman responsible for killin' two hired hands workin' for Thomas Frazer. We're also lookin' for a wanted murderer named Todd Moony, who was last seen near Rockbed."

"Well, I'm afraid I cannot help you there," Boon replied. "I built this ranch to shield myself from the struggles of the world and society. If somebody sought to hide here, someone would likely shoot them on sight as trespassers."

"So you haven't seen them?" Carsten asked.

"Nope." Boon shook his head. "I'm sorry to have wasted your time, Marshal McNeil."

"I ain't so sure." Carsten stared at him. "The two fellas who got bushwhacked last night spoke to me 'bout a range war in these parts. They also mentioned somethin' 'bout somebody by the name of Amy Filmore bein' held against her will in a compound in the area. Perhaps you'd care to enlighten me?"

"Those are some very serious allegations, mister." Boon scowled at Carsten. "None of the Frazer hands have been here, so what they said could be considered libelous. You're not welcome on my property unless you have a search warrant."

"Very well." Carsten tipped his hat. He turned his horse around and rode down the trail.

Nastas followed behind. Boon gestured for the guards to shut the gates. He walked back to the house. Hank sat at the table with his arms folded and scowled at Boon as he sat back down.

"My apologies for the interruption," Boon said. "But it seems someone in Mr. Frazer's employ has divulged information about my operation. I cannot allow that to be known, especially to a US Marshal. Now, how do you think they would have learned of that?" He jabbed his walking stick into Hank's chest.

Hank gulped, and Reid cracked his knuckles. The sound made Hank flinch. "I don't know!" he spluttered. "If it was Frazer's boys, I wouldn't have had anythin' to do with it!"

"It's your call, Mr. Boon," Reid said.

Boon lowered the walking stick. "I believe you, for now. But you need to keep quiet about this. Our business has concluded. Are we in agreement?"

Hank gave a curt nod. He stood up.

"However..." Boon held the stick on the porch rail to block Hank's path. "If you speak about this to anybody, especially the lawman, your family will bury you on the prairie. Remember that. Because I'll know." He snapped his fingers to a ranch hand wandering the yard. "Show Mr. Patterson to the gates."

Hank mounted his horse and followed the ranch hand out of the compound.

"Please take a seat, Mr. Reid." Boon sat down and gestured to the vacant chair. "There's something I'd like to ask you about."

"Fine." Reid sat down. "What do you need?"

"Does the name Carsten McNeil mean anything to you? You seemed to recognize it when the guard at the gate mentioned him."

"There's no gunfighter in this territory who doesn't know Quaker McNeil."

"Why do they call him Quaker?" Boon gave a small chuckle. "He's in the wrong business if he's a Quaker."

"In his first gunfight, he shot a man in the hand. And he never wants to have a showdown unless he has to. I guess that's why he became a lawman instead of a bounty hunter. He wants to take people alive."

Boon leaned toward the table. He clasped his hands.

"Do you want me to take care of him?"

"No. Not yet. I imagine you'll want to prove your mettle as a gunfighter by killing the legendary Quaker McNeil. You'll get your chance soon enough. I'm still trying to piece together how he learned about Miss Filmore."

"Blaine Weber. That's my best guess. She might have given him a note."

"If that's the case," Boon replied, "then he's going to come back eventually. And if he comes back, he'll have a warrant. He was also looking for Todd Moony. We need to hide Mr. Moony and Miss Filmore. If he does come by and suspects nothing further, he'll ride on."

"And if he doesn't ride on?" Reid leaned closer.

"Then you can have your attempt at being a legend." Boon sat back.

"I doubt he'll want a showdown."

"Convince him. You said yourself he won't have a gunfight without a reason. Find one. And if all else fails, you can always shoot him in the back."

Chapter 15
Taking Stock

The clock in the foyer struck twelve. Carsten and his deputies sat in the dining room of the hotel in Rockbed. A plate of steak and potatoes lay untouched in front of Carsten. The other tables sat unoccupied.

"Carsten?" Fleur tapped him on the shoulder. "Aren't you hungry?"

"Sorry, I was just thinkin'." Carsten picked up his cutlery. "Todd Moony is still at large. Blaine Weber is likely dead. And we've got two other bodies on our hands. I'm wonderin' what this Mr. Boon fella is involved in. "How did it go with Mr. Patterson?"

"He wasn't there," Fleur replied. "But we met Harvey's three friends. They made it back to the ranch last night, and they didn't have their guns."

"They came by earlier to collect them from the sheriff's office and take that Harvey fella back," Wilkins added. "None of them used a Sharps but that don't exactly suggest one of them didn't kill the Frazer boys."

"Nastas figured from the tracks that the killer was on his lonesome," Clifford said.

"We can agree on that." Carsten chewed a piece of steak. "I reckon Mr. Boon is pourin' coal oil on this fire that's burnin' between Patterson and Frazer. I'm tryin' to figure out what end he has in mind."

"Where did the trail of the killer lead?" Fleur asked.

"It took us near the Boon spread," Carsten replied. "But we didn't get past the gate. I'm gonna need to wire the judge and see if'n we can get a search warrant."

"How do we prove that?" Fleur said. "The people who told us have been killed and we don't have any evidence to go on."

"The telegraph office in Globe might have somethin'." Carsten massaged his temples. "That fella, rest his soul, mentioned sending a telegram to Boston. I just wonder if Mr. Filmore ever got the message."

"You think Boon's shelterin' outlaws?" Clifford asked.

"Maybe," Carsten said.

A creaky floorboard prompted the conversation to fall silent. A waitress approached the table with a steaming pot. "Can I get anybody some more coffee?" she asked.

"That would be much appreciated, ma'am." Carsten smiled. He nodded as she refilled his cup. "You get many Patterson or Frazer hands in this place?"

"Not really," she replied. "Most of them go to the saloon. They prefer the… company there. To be honest, you and your deputies are the most guests we've had since we opened."

"Well, maybe if things become more peaceful, that'll change," Carsten said.

"I hope so." The waitress smiled. "Let me know if you need anything else." She walked back to the kitchen.

"Something else is troubling you, isn't it?" Fleur placed a hand on Carsten's shoulder.

"Whoever bushwhacked Al and Roy must have known 'bout what they shared with us," Carsten said. "Word must have gotten back to Mr. Boon somehow."

"I wondered that, too." Clifford stared at the other deputies. "You think someone tipped him off?"

Knives and forks clattered at his remark. Wilkins, Moses, and Nastas all stared in Clifford's direction.

"Is that true, Marshal?" Wilkins said. "Do you really suspect us after all we've been through?"

"I don't wanna think 'bout that," Carsten said. "Have any of y'all been to Rockbed before?"

"Can't say that I have," Clifford said. "I've been raised in Phoenix all my life."

"We shouldn't be distrustful of each other." Fleur stood up. "Boon might have bribed or intimidated most of the townsfolk here. Any of them could have tipped him off. None of us have been to Rockbed before and none of us have family in Rockbed. So we don't have a reason to suspect one another."

"I agree," Clifford said. "If we start fightin' among ourselves, Mr. Boon will be the only one who stands to gain."

"The tenderfoot's right," Wilkins said. "Boon wants to divide us. The same way he's dividin' Patterson and Frazer, I reckon."

"So that's settled." Carsten smiled at Clifford and Fleur. They smiled back. "We ought to finish up and figure out what our next move is."

***

After lunch, the posse left the hotel and returned to the sheriff's office.

"Clifford, I need you and Nastas to ride back to Globe and check with the telegraph office." Carsten sat at the desk. "See if he knows 'bout the wire sent to Boston. I also need you to wire Judge Stanley in Phoenix. Tell him 'bout the situation and that I'm gonna need a search warrant for the Boon ranch."

"What evidence should I use?" Clifford asked.

"I reckon the telegram sent to Mr. Filmore should provide the evidence we need," Carsten said. "That'll prove Miss Filmore is tryin' to reach him."

"Right, Marshal." Clifford nodded. "When do we head out?"

"Now," Carsten replied.

Nastas led Clifford outside.

"Carsten, I have a question." Fleur sat down at one chair opposite the desk.

"Go ahead," he replied.

"Clifford suggested something about Boon sheltering outlaws. What do you make of that?"

"That fit in with what Bowman Ratcliff said on his way to Yuma," Wilkins added.

Moses nodded in agreement.

"I'm startin' to believe it." Carsten fidgeted. "He mentioned a compound. Perhaps he's providin' a safe haven for many outlaws."

"Do you think he's doing something similar to Sheriff Garrett?" Fleur asked.

"You might be onto somethin' there, darlin'." Carsten stood up and paced around the office. "That compound would be the perfect place to house a band of outlaws. And by offerin' them a hideout, you got them in your pocket. You can send them to steal in another county where the sheriffs can't chase 'em. But a fella's gonna get real antsy without vices, so you set up a cantina on your own ranch."

"Do you reckon Blaine Weber was hidin' there?" Wilkins rested his foot on Carsten's vacant chair.

"If he was, then what was he doin' in Rockbed if there's a cantina at the ranch?" Moses stroked his chin. "Was he lookin' for the compound, or did he sneak out?"

"Would you want your hard-earned dollars goin' back into the pockets of your boss?" Wilkins replied.

"I also think some people can become irritable when they're stuck in one place for too long," Fleur added. "I know I've been finding that while living in Phoenix."

"I reckon you're right, darlin'," Carsten said. "Maybe Blaine was feelin' cooped up and snuck out. Maybe he complained 'bout it to Miss Filmore, and she snuck him that note, thinkin' she had an opportunity to escape. I reckon that Norman Reid fella went after him in case the operation got exposed by his illicit night out."

"But where does that leave us?" Fleur asked.

"That's the real question," Carsten said. "Unless we find that note, we can't prove nothin'. We'd have to wire the prison warden in Yuma to see if Bowman Ratcliff could confirm that story. But then we'd need to wire the judge if he accepts some kind of bargain. Who knows how long that'll take?"

The other deputies fell silent. Fleur stared toward the cells. Carsten walked over to Willie Snow's cell. The sheriff dozed on the cot. An empty plate sat on the floor nearby.

"Sheriff?" Carsten said.

"I've been listenin' in this whole time." Snow stared at the ceiling. "If you're askin' me to confess, you're wastin' your breath."

"Care for a cigar?" Carsten held one up.

"Sure." Snow lifted himself out of the cot. He pushed the empty plate beneath the cell door with his foot.

"Here." Carsten lit the cigar and passed it through the bars.

"Much obliged." Snow drew smoke from the cigar and lay back on the cot.

"I'm gonna waste my breath, like you said," Carsten began. "If'n you give me somethin' that implicates Mr. Boon, you can go free. I don't see good chances of you carryin' on to be a lawman, but I can help you find some other work."

"What good is that when you're dead?" Snow replied. "You ever heard of Demon Eyes Reid?"

"I heard stories." Carsten said. "He's quite the gun hand. He's got warrants out in New Mexico and Wyoming, along with Texas, so I reckon I'll be servin' one on him sooner or later."

"Good luck with that." Snow chuckled. "He once killed a man for snorin' and plenty more for breathin'."

"Let me guess…" Carsten leaned against the wall. "He's gonna be comin' after you if'n Boon finds out you talked."

"More likely, he's gonna be comin' after you." Snow stared at the young marshal. "I heard 'bout your reputation, Quaker McNeil. You bested that lethal limey back in Yavapai County. What was the fella's name? Oh yeah, English Bill Harvey. When you have a reputation, you won't have to find Reid. He'll find you. And your reluctance to fight won't save you. Stay here, and you'll be puttin' a lot of your friends at risk of an early grave. Like that tenderfoot kid. Or perhaps even Mrs. McNeil."

Carsten felt his heart clench.

"That thought hurts, don't it?" Snow laughed.

"You're afraid too," Carsten replied as he stepped back into the office.

His deputies stared at him.

"Marshal?" Wilkins forced a smile.

Carsten opened his mouth to speak.

"We heard everything." Fleur embraced him. "Don't let him get to you."

He nodded and returned the embrace.

"Do you think Reid's at that compound, too?" Moses asked.

"I reckon so," Carsten replied. "So y'all had best watch yourselves."

"I'm not going anywhere," Fleur said. "I know you're afraid to lose me and I'm afraid to lose you. But I know the risks of being with you. It may not come to this."

"How far is Globe from here?" Carsten said.

"Couple hours' ride by my reckoning," Wilkins said. "With any luck, Clifford and Nastas should be back by noon tomorrow."

***

The following morning, Carsten rose from his bed in the hotel. He smiled at Fleur as she continued to doze.

"What's the plan for today?" she murmured.

"I reckon we wait around." Carsten reached for his boots. "Keep patrol in the town. Might as well keep the peace while we're here."

After breakfast, the couple returned to the sheriff's office. Two riders appeared on the horizon.

"Is that…" Fleur began.

"Yup," Carsten replied. "Clifford and Nastas. Wasn't expectin' 'em back so soon."

The two deputies trotted to the sheriff's office. They hitched their horses. A sweat drenched Clifford slid out of his saddle and splashed himself with water from the horse trough.

"You thirsty, deputy?" Carsten grinned.

"I'll say." Clifford nodded. "Keepin' up with your tracker is a real endurance test."

"Well, you managed it," Carsten said. "Why don't you come inside and get yourself some coffee? Then we can talk about what you brought back."

Inside, Clifford fanned himself with his hat. The smell of sweat and horse dander filled the room in the heat. "Looks like the judge was ahead of us," Clifford said. "A wire got sent to your office yesterday. All the way from Boston, too."

"Boston?" Carsten's eyebrow raised. "Let me guess, Filmore?"

"Right." Clifford nodded. "Turns out Mr. Fillmore had a real terrible argument with his sister, and she left to be a mail-order bride and disappeared soon after. He got the message a couple weeks back about bein' held in the compound. They passed the wire on to the judge after he sent it to your office. He reached into his pocket and produced the telegram.

"This is great." Carsten skimmed through it. "Now we've got evidence."

"This also came through." Clifford produced another sheet of paper. "Hand delivered."

Carsten smiled as he unfolded it and saw the judge's signature at the bottom of the page.

"What's the plan?" Fleur asked.

"We've got our warrant," Carsten said. "You, Wilkins, and Brennan will ride with me. Clifford and Nastas can have some loafin' time."

Chapter 16
Nothing out of the Ordinary

The shutters in Boon's office did little to ease the stifling heat. Boon sat at his desk, looking through bills. Shadow bathed the room except for the area covered by the one oil lamp on the desk. A knock on the door caught his attention. "Who is it?" he called.

"It's me," Norman replied from outside the room.

Boon picked up the lamp and opened the door.

"The sentry is saying Marshal McNeil is at the gates. And he's got a search warrant."

"Son of a…" Boon muttered under his breath. "He mustn't suspect anything. Get Todd and anybody else who's wanted and hide them. Take Miss Filmore there too. I suspect he'll be looking specifically for her."

"What about the four Mexican girls?"

"They know to keep quiet," Boon replied. "It's in their interest."

Boon shielded himself from the sunlight as he stepped outside. He made his way to the compound gates. Outside the compound, Carsten sat on horseback, accompanied by three other deputies, one of whom was missing an arm and another who was a woman.

"My apologies for keeping you waiting, Marshal McNeil." Boon tipped his hat. "I was engrossed in some financial matters. Anyway, it's nice of you to visit again. What can I do for you?"

"Mr. Boon." Carsten dismounted. "I'd like to look around your compound. I got a warrant signed by Federal Judge Arma Stanley, which gives me the legal authority to do so." He handed the letter over to Boon.

"Can I ask on what grounds this is based?" Boon said.

"Allegations of kidnappin'," Carsten said.

"Those are some interesting claims." Boon chuckled.

"They sure are," Carsten replied. "Claims or not, you gotta let me in, or we can charge you with contempt of court or obstruction of justice."

"Then I'd better let you in," Boon replied with a beckoning gesture. "You can hitch your horses by the house."

Carsten led his horse through the gates, followed by his deputies. Boon led them along the courtyard. Ranch hands tipped hats as they passed by. One group played horseshoes by the barn.

"We initially built these fortifications to protect my employees in the event of any Apache incursions," Boon said. "A man can't be too careful in these parts."

"I suppose not." Carsten tethered his horse to a hitching post. "What kinda ranch do you run here, Mr. Boon? Cattle? Sheep?"

"I'm mainly in cattle," Boon replied. "But I have a pasture that's better suited to grazing sheep. As I have no sheep of my own, I offer it to the local sheep farmers."

"Like the Patterson and Frazer outfits?" Carsten asked.

"Yes," Boon said in a sullen tone. "It's unfortunate they had to descend into their feud, which resulted in lives being taken. I see no reason for it. My pasture was open to both of them."

"You mind if we look inside the barn?" Carsten gestured toward it. "That could be a great place to hide."

"Your warrant permits it," Boon said. He led the posse inside the barn. The smell of horse manure in the heat caused him to gag. "Can you make this search quickly so we don't have to spend too long in here?"

Carsten said nothing. He wandered through the barn and climbed into the hayloft. Boon listened to the marshal's boots on the ladder and in the loft.

"All clear," Carsten said after what seemed like ages.

***

The late afternoon sun cast shadows across the compound as the deputies neared the end of their search.

"As you can see," Boon said, "there was nothing out of the ordinary in the house, the barn, the bunkhouse, or the storehouses. Before you leave, I'd like to show you I've saved the best part for last."

The marshals followed him to the single-story adobe structure near the bunkhouse.

"It's a situation the world over that ranch hands will cause no small amount of chaos when they've been paid," Boon said. "They get drunk, they get into petty arguments over cards or women. Then the saloonkeepers will put pressure on me to reel them in. But I have no intention of depriving my employees of the vices they crave. So I came up with an alternative: an on-site cantina open to all my ranch hands." He beckoned the deputies to enter the cantina.

A man in a soiled derby hat stood behind a bar with bottles of whiskey and tequila. Four Mexican women in threadbare dresses loitered in the room.

"Would you folks like something to drink?" Boon gestured to the bartender. He produced four glasses.

"Not while we're on duty." Carsten raised a hand.

"You don't drink?" Boon grinned.

"I do," Carsten replied. "I'm just not drinkin' now. I ain't never heard of a ranch with its own cantina. Especially with some workin' girls. Where do you hire them from?"

"I can offer you a free service from one of them—" Boon said.

"I'm married," Carsten interrupted. "And I ain't here for that. So I'd like an answer to the question if you don't mind. How did you four ladies come into your employment?"

"I have contracts of employment back in my office," Boon said.

"I'm askin' the ladies," Carsten said. "Is what he sayin' true? Does he have contracts drawn up for y'all?"

One woman looked at Boon. He stared at her. She nodded, avoiding eye contact with Carsten.

"You see?" Boon said. "There's nothing for you to be concerned about. These girls came across the border willingly in search of gainful employment, in what we call the oldest profession. Is there anything else you wish to know?"

Carsten exchanged a glance with his three deputies. "I think we're finished here." He tipped his hat. "You have a good day now, Mr. Boon. Thanks for takin' the time to oblige us. We'll see ourselves out."

Boon watched the gates shut. He returned to the barn and opened a trapdoor concealed beneath the hay in one stall. "It's safe to come out." He tapped his walking stick.

Reid emerged from the hidden cellar accompanied by Todd Moony and Amy Filmore, along with a couple of other men. Todd led Amy back toward the cantina.

"Do you think he's convinced?" Reid asked as he walked with Boon toward the house.

"That boy is no fool," Boon replied. "I need you to head into Rockbed and keep an eye on him. See if he rides on or not."

"And if he doesn't?" Reid tapped the Schofield revolvers in his holster.

"Then Marshal McNeil has overstayed his welcome in my town. And you can finally get that showdown you seem to itch for."

Chapter 17
The Revelation

"What did you make of Mr. Boon?" Fleur asked Carsten as they trotted along the trail back to Rockbed.

"I reckon he's a good liar," Carsten replied. "If he's hidin' Todd Moony and Miss Filmore, he's done a real good job. But that Mexican girl wasn't as convincin' for him."

"What do you mean by that?" Wilkins asked.

"She was afraid," Fleur replied.

"Mr. Boon might have spun a tall yarn 'bout contracts," Carsten said, "but the fear in that woman's eyes suggested otherwise. It's likely they had threatened her into keepin' silent."

"Those poor women..." Fleur tightened her grip on the reins. "Maybe we should try raiding. Could we claim Todd Moony has been tracked to the ranch?"

"We should have done that first," Carsten said. "And we'd need an army to do a thing like that."

"Should we wire for more deputies from Globe?" Wilkins asked.

"We'll have to think 'bout this," Carsten said. "The warrant turned up nothin', so we need to ask the judge again."

***

They hitched their horses outside the marshal's office in Rockbed.

Clifford peered out from the door. "Marshal McNeil? How did it go at the Boon spread?"

"No sign of Todd Moony or Miss Filmore." Carsten dismounted. "But I met some of the Mexican girls who are working on the ranch, and I got reason to believe they're bein' held against their will."

"Well, there's a fella by the name of Patterson who wants to speak to you," Clifford said. "He's waitin' inside."

Carsten's eyebrows rose. "I think I might want to hear this." He hurried inside.

Hank Patterson sat on one chair in front of the desk. He fidgeted with his thumbs.

"Mr. Patterson?" Carsten extended his hand. "I'm Carsten McNeil, US Marshal for the Arizona Territory. Sorry to keep you waitin'. How can I be of service?"

"I'm in over my head, and I've just been ripped off." Hank accepted the handshake but didn't look at Carsten. "I'd heard the sheriff got thrown into his own calaboose, so I figured I'd speak to you."

"Who ripped you off and what happened?" Carsten sat down behind the desk. He looked Hank over. The ranch owner kept peering over his shoulder toward the door.

"A while back"—Hank gestured for Carsten to lean closer—"Milt Boon's hands began demanding tolls on the sheepherders passin' through his land to get to the pasture. I tried gettin' the sheriff, but he's pretty much in Boon's pocket."

"I figured that out already." Carsten rested his feet on the desk.

"What's he in jail for?" Hank asked.

"Obstruction of justice. He denied knowledge of the whereabouts of a wanted fugitive, but then a witness sighted them ridin' together. Anyhow, what happened next?"

"Boon sent his foreman to bring me back to his spread. That's when I found out 'bout his cantina."

"Did you see Miss Filmore while you were there?"

"I did." Hank nodded. "She tried to give me a letter but had to hide it when Boon came by. Boon wanted Frazer's land. He offered me twenty head of cattle if I could drive Frazer away. I've always wanted to get into the cattle business. Seems more lucrative than sheep. But Boon went back on my deal and threatened me if I talked."

"You agreed to start a feud for a few steers?" Carsten stood up and loomed over Hank. "I ain't even heard of anythin' that low. I ought to have you arrested as an accomplice unless you can offer me somethin' real good."

"Sheep farmin' ain't always the best." Hank buried his head in his hands. "With Boon's tolls, I can barely afford to keep on my hired help. My boy Aaron is supposed to inherit my land when I go. But I wanted the place to be in a fit state."

The doors to the office opened. Wilkins and Moses entered with a white-bearded man. Carsten winced as an overpowering smell of bourbon filled the room. The man swayed as he stood, forcing Moses to support him.

"We used to knock," Carsten said.

"Sorry, Marshal," Wilkins replied. "This fella got thrown out of the saloon, so we figured we'd take him in for bein' drunk and disorderly."

"Frazer?" Hank looked over at the newcomer.

The man stared back and seemed to appear sober for a moment.

"Mr. Thomas Frazer, I'm guessin'?" Carsten put his hands together. "Looks like fate has delivered you to me. Please, sit yourself down before you fall over."

"Where's the chef?" Frazer slurred as he flopped into the other vacant chair. "Why's that coyote Patterson here?"

"He's here because he's made a confession," Carsten replied, "that he was in cahoots with Milt Boon to steal your land away from you. Seems Mr. Boon figured he could square you off 'gainst each other while presentin' himself as the guy who brokers peace."

"What did that weasel promise you?" Frazer said with a cacophonous belch.

"He promised him cattle," Carsten said. "After—"

"You Judas Iscariot!" Frazer lunged at Hank but fell to the floor in a crumpled heap.

Carsten stood up. He prodded him with his foot. "Help him back up," he said to Hank. "Clifford, is there any coffee left?"

Hank nodded. He lifted Frazer's arm as Carsten took the other arm. They heaved the drunk rancher upward and placed him back in the chair. Clifford handed over a cup of coffee. Frazer took it and downed the contents, spilling the majority down his shirt.

"Don't worry," Clifford said. "It was lukewarm anyhow."

"You've sold your land?" Carsten asked.

"Boon made an offer for my land," Frazer said. "I just wanted to leave before any more of my hands were killed."

"If that's the case…" Carsten turned to Hank. "I reckon Boon will be gunnin' for you next. He's already ripped you off with that cattle deal. Maybe he'll pull the same thing."

"Boon has a lot of gunmen workin' his spread," Hank replied. "You might be right there, Marshal."

"I've heard enough." Carsten sat down. "It's plain to me that Milt Boon has played you from the start. It seems mighty convenient he offered to buy the land when this feud reared its ugly head. I got reason to believe he's shelterin' outlaws and is involved in some kind of prostitution ring."

"That sounds about right," Hank replied. "Boon talked about takin' in wanted outlaws and offerin' them a second chance. That's why he offered me the cattle. In exchange, I wouldn't speak 'bout this with anybody."

"I'll make you a deal," Carsten said. "If you want to get out of this, put your feud with Thomas Frazer behind you and testify against Milt Boon in court. If'n we can find any of his outlaws, we can put him away for a long time if the judge decides not to give him a hemp necktie. I'll speak to the judge on your behalf."

"You're gonna try to arrest Milt Boon?" Frazer cackled. "You're either mighty brave or mighty stupid, mister. He's got at least thirty men on his spread. And some of them are wanted for murderer. How many deputies have you got? Five?"

"I can get more," Carsten said. "But you're gonna have to stay somewhere secure. I can sequester you in the hotel. They got plenty of rooms."

"Even if you kept him in Yuma Territorial Prison, Demon Eyes will still get to him." Frazer laughed.

"You finished?" Carsten said. "Because Milt Boon ain't the first cattle baron I went against. 'Bout four years back, there was a fella by the name of Moraday who moved to Yavapai County and sought to buy up the town of Cripple Gorge, along with all the ranches. That included my pa's. He wouldn't sell, and some real difficulty brewed. Moraday's men robbed my ma. They burned our barn while we were all at church. They tried pickin' a fight with me and Pa in the general store. When that didn't work, he poisoned our waterin' hole, set me up to be killed in a showdown, and then kidnapped my sister. But my brother, our friends, and my future wife banded together and saved her. In the process, I shot and killed Moraday. Milt Boon don't scare me, and neither does Demon Eyes. But if'n you want to fix this, you gotta work together."

A silence filled the room. Hank and Frazer exchanged glances.

"Truce?" Hank extended his hand.

"Truce." Frazer lifted his own arm.

Hank grabbed the hand as it flopped toward him. Carsten smiled as he watched them shake hands. The other deputies clapped. Wilkins placed his fingers in his mouth and whistled.

"So what's the plan?" Fleur said.

"We're gonna head to Globe and send a wire to Phoenix," Carsten replied. "We'll need reinforcements. Fleur, you'll ride with me. The rest of you, keep things orderly 'round here. Mr. Patterson and Mr. Frazer should be kept in the hotel. I suspect if Boon finds out what's happenin', he'll try somethin'. Perhaps he's got someone in town to tip him off, as well as the sheriff. You'd best be ready."

"Right, Marshal." Wilkins nodded.

"We'd best mount up." Carsten donned his hat. "We should be back by mornin'."

***

The sun was setting as Carsten and Fleur arrived in Globe.

"Who do you think we'll be able to recruit?" Fleur asked. "It'll take a week for people to arrive from Phoenix."

"If we can't recruit nobody in Globe," Carsten said, "we might get some folk from Superior or any of the other surrounding burgs."

They hitched their horses outside the telegraph office. Carsten stepped inside, greeted by the smell of oil.

A man in a green visor sat behind a desk, with a telegraph machine behind him. "Can I help you, son?" He stood up. "Just pony up. I want to go home."

"It's real urgent." Carsten revealed his US Marshal's badge. "I need you to send a wire out to Phoenix. Tell them US Marshal Carsten McNeil is requesting any available deputies to meet me in Rockbed. I'm raisin' a posse."

"How many do wish to send?" The operator picked up a pencil and paper.

"Send them to all offices in Pinal, Gila, and Maricopa Counties," Carsten said.

The operator spun his chair around. He tapped away at the key.

Carsten watched the machine working. "Let's hope they can arrive real soon." Carsten placed some money on the counter. "Let me know if I'm short. If I ain't, keep the change." He tipped his hat and left.

Fleur waited by the hitching post.

"That's done," he said. "Now we can check if there are any deputies here."

They walked over to a stone building signposted as the marshal's office.

"Well, well, well." A woman in a wide-brimmed hat and duster coat walked out of the office. "If it ain't the leprechaun cowboy."

Carsten rolled his eyes at the remark.

"Leprechaun?" Fleur mouthed.

"Only one person calls me that," Carsten replied. "It's good to see you again, Ramona." He extended his hand.

"Ramona Vasquez?" Fleur said.

"Nice to see you're moving up in the world, Señora McNeil." Ramona stared at her deputy badge, ignoring Carsten's hand.

"It took the judge some convincin'," Carsten replied. "Who are lookin' for this time?"

"Just brought in Dirty Dan Stanton." Ramona gestured to the office with her thumb. "Or rather, a corpse with his strong resemblance. Who are you after?"

"Todd Moony," Carsten said. "And I know where he's hidin'."

"Just tell me, and I'll bring him back." Ramona folded her arms.

"You go in there alone, and we'll be ferryin' your corpse back to town." Carsten wagged a finger. "He's hidin' in a compound owned by a cattle baron with the handle of Boon. That big bug's got himself an army, so I'm here to recruit some deputies. Do you want to ride with me?"

"Are there any bounties on the other folks?" Ramona raised an eyebrow.

"I reckon so," Carsten said. "You'll get your share. But watch where you shoot. Boon's got a couple workin' girls he's holdin' against their will."

"I'll ride with you." Ramona shook Carsten's hand.

"Much obliged." Carsten tipped his hat. "I'm gonna see if I can recruit some more deputies. The more I can get, the better." He stepped inside the marshal's office.

Three men with deputy badges loitered around the desks.

"Evenin' fellas." Carsten showed his own badge. "By the powers invested in me by the Arizona Territory, I'm recruitin' you for a federal posse."

"Who are ya goin' after?" one deputy asked.

"We're raidin' a compound that is shelterin' wanted outlaws owned by a fella, the name of Milt Boon," Carsten replied. "They've also been involved in some kinda slavery ring, kidnappin' women and makin' 'em workin' girls. We're ridin' to Rockbed at dawn."

"You heard him, boys," one deputy said. "Get the rifles from the cabinet."

Chapter 18
An Affair of Honor

Dawn rose the following day. Carsten and Fleur rode back to Rockbed, accompanied by Ramona and the deputies from Globe.

"Carsten…" Fleur brought her horse alongside his. "What's the business with the leprechaun cowboy? Where did it come from?"

"It was when we were goin' after Wiley Frye's gang 'bout three years back," Carsten replied. "I got into a shootout and held my own 'fore the rest of the posse arrived. They shot quite a few bullets at me while I was crouched behind some rocks. My coat picked up a few holes, but I didn't take any hits. I don't believe it either, if you're wonderin'."

"That's another story you've never shared." Fleur cracked a smile.

"It's because he's embarrassed by the nickname," Ramona said from behind them.

The Globe deputies laughed.

"I hear you shot a fella through his mask in the courthouse," one deputy commented.

"I did what I had to," Carsten replied. "I don't like killin' if'n I can help it."

"But most of the hombres you chase are wanted for hangin' offenses," Ramona said. "Even if you bring them in alive, they'll only swing. They have no reason to work with you. That's why they're called desperados. They're desperate men, and there's never a more dangerous threat."

"But there has to be law and justice," Carsten said. "It ain't my job to be judge, jury, and executioner. We have a constitution, don't we?"

"That don't matter much in these parts." Ramona sneered. "What's stopping a guilty fella gettin' found innocent, then lookin' for payback?"

Carsten fell silent for a minute. "My pa quit his badge after he killed a man while foilin' a stagecoach robbery." He exhaled. "The man's three brothers and a cousin raided our farm. We fought them off, but our hired hand was killed and Pa took a bullet in the leg and will never walk properly again. I was fourteen years old. I'd already taken lives when I took my badge and oath. But Pa made me swear I'd never start a gunfight, only finish it."

The riders trotted up Rockbed's main street as the townspeople stared at them. Some retreated into their homes or shops. Carsten hitched his horse outside the sheriff's office.

"What's the plan?" Ramona asked.

"I'm gonna wait a couple of days for more deputies to arrive," Carsten replied. "Sheriff here's been charged with obstruction and is languishin' in one of his own cells. I also got two witnesses sequestered in the hotel. They all need to be guarded, so we're workin' in shifts." He stepped inside the office.

A well-dressed man with three scars and a perpetual frown sat behind the desk. "So you're the famous Marshal McNeil." He struck a match on the desk and lit a cigar.

"And you must be Demon Eyes Reid," Carsten replied. "What are you doin' here?"

"I understand someone have unlawfully detained the sheriff," Reid said. "I've been appointed as his deputy and have detained the man responsible. He's languishin' in the cell." The last sentence was said in a way to mimic Carsten's drawl.

Carsten reached for his Remington.

"I wouldn't do that if I were you." Reid stood up. He produced a bundle of dynamite from beneath the desk. He held the cigar close to the fuse. "One false move and I'll blow you all into the next county."

"Someone check the cells." Carsten maintained his stare on Reid. "I wanna know what's happenin'."

Fleur stepped inside and disappeared into the cell block. "Snow's dead!" she called out. "Clifford's in another cell. He's alive, but in awful shape!"

"You killed the sheriff?" Carsten asked.

"He had become a liability to Mr. Boon," Reid said. "That's what happens to liabilities. I believe Mr. Patterson and Mr. Frazer are in the hotel with your other three deputies?"

"They'll kill you," Carsten said. "That deputy you beat up is the judge's nephew."

"And he's not cut out for this line of work." Reid sneered. "Unlike you. I know who you are, Quaker McNeil. You're quite the legend in these parts. I'm calling you out, mister."

"Hold on there…" Carsten raised his hands.

"You'd better make your choice." Reid touched the cigar against the fuse. It sparked.

Fleur reached for her gun as Reid reached for his.

"Wait!" Carsten raised his hand.

They both stopped. Their hands rested on their pistol grips. The fuse continued to hiss. Fleur and Carsten exchanged glances with Reid.

"You don't have to do this," Carsten said. "I'll meet you outside."

"A wise decision." Reid snuffed out the fuse with a gloved hand. "You had better make your peace with your wife there." He stepped outside.

Carsten saw Fleur's hand tremble. "I'm sorry, darlin'." He embraced her. "I don't like these showdowns, but ain't gonna put nobody else's life in danger like that. I didn't start this fight, but I'm gonna finish it."

"You'll defeat him." Tears welled in her eyes. "I know you will."

"I'm hopin' so." He nodded and walked toward the door.

"Carsten?" Fleur said.

He stopped at the door. "Yes, darlin'?"

"Can you promise you'll come back from this?"

"I hate breakin' promises." He closed his eyes. "So I ain't gonna make that one. It's the gunslinger's curse."

"What do you mean?"

"When I had a showdown with English Bill all those years ago…" Carsten turned back and rested his hands on his wife's shoulders. "He said with his dyin' words that for as long as I'm breathin', there'll be fellas lookin' to beat me to the draw hoping that killin' me will cement their own legend. One day there's gonna be a day when I won't be faster on the draw. Nobody is the fastest gun in the west forever."

"I see." She bowed her head.

"Quaker McNeil!" Reid shouted from outside. "You'd better get out here right now!"

"But not today." Carsten stroked her chin. "If'n I live through this, I'm gonna retire." Carsten stepped outside.

Reid stood in the middle of the street. The other deputies kept their weapons trained on him. Wilkins, Moses, and Nastas ran out of the hotel with their guns drawn.

"Lower your weapons!" Carsten said. "There are too many bystanders. I reckon this is gonna have to be some kind of affair of honor."

"You'd best not keep me waitin', McNeil," Reid snarled.

"I was just writin' out my will," Carsten replied. He stepped to the opposite end of the street.

A silence fell on the town, save for the cawing of a passing bird. Reid glared at Carsten. Carsten felt his own heartbeat as he limbered his fingers.

"You know you're outnumbered?" Carsten hollered. "Soon as you kill me, my deputies are likely to shoot you down and say you resisted arrest."

"That doesn't bother me," Reid said. "Even if I die today, I'd like to be known as the man who killed Quaker McNeil."

"You and every other two-bit wannabe." Carsten grinned. "Ready when you are."

"Draw." Reid said with a sharpness as cutting as his stare.

Carsten's Remington left his holster. Two shots echoed through the street. A bullet punched into his arm. He spun to the ground.

"Carsten!" Fleur screamed. She ran out toward him.

"Wait!" Carsten shouted. He looked ahead.

His opponent remained standing. He aimed his revolver. Carsten took a deep breath. Reid's arm swung down. He dropped to his knees. His Schofield slid out of his fingers, and he slumped forward. The townspeople ran toward Reid's body.

"Carsten?" Fleur ran over to him, accompanied by the other deputies.

"I'm fine." He clenched his teeth as he gripped his wounded arm. "Looks like the bullet just grazed me."

"That was a close one." She helped him to his feet.

"Amen to that," Carsten replied. He walked over to Reid's body and kicked dust over him. "Come on, let's get inside and see to Clifford."

"Sure." Fleur embraced him, but withdrew as he grimaced. "Sorry."

"Is there a doctor in this town?" Carsten yelled to the onlookers.

"Me!" One man raised his hand. "Well, kind of. I'm a barber."

"It'll have to do," Carsten murmured to Fleur, who cracked a smile.

The couple entered the sheriff's office. Carsten walked over to the cell Clifford occupied. The deputy lay on the cot. He sported a black eye and several bruises, along with swollen lips. Fleur unlocked the door.

"Marshal..." Clifford said in a weak voice. "I'm sorry. He just came in here and held me at gunpoint. He pistol-whipped me a couple times, then locked me in that cell."

"It ain't your fault," Carsten replied. "What happened next?"

"He unlocked the sheriff's cell." Clifford raised his arm and pointed at the opposite cell.

Carsten turned around. Snow lay slumped against the wall. He noticed a stab wound in the man's stomach.

"He stuck a knife in his belly," Clifford said. "But he was breathin' for a real long time afterward."

"When did this happen?" Carsten kneeled by the cot.

"Just after sunup," Clifford said. "I was waitin' to be relieved. He turned to me. He wanted to know where you were, and I said you'd be comin' back soon."

The barber entered the office door with a leather satchel. "Who's hurt?"

"My deputy," Carsten said. "He's been beat up pretty bad. Plus, my arm's lettin' in the air."

"Well, you'd best get it cleaned and dressed," the barber replied.

"What kind of barber doubles as a doctor?" Fleur asked.

"I worked as an orderly in a field hospital," the barber replied. "Ended up opening a barbershop in Rockbed after getting mustered out. Became a pretty good dentist too. Before the Patterson and Frazer feud, I was pulling out more teeth than bullets."

"Well, I reckon we're both in excellent hands," Carsten said.

***

The following morning, Carsten woke up in his hotel room with Fleur by his side. He looked at his bandaged arm. He smiled as he stroked her hair. She smiled back and woke up.

"What are our plans?" she asked. "How will we attack the ranch?"

"We need to wait," he said. "See if'n we can get more deputies." He heaved himself out of bed.

"How's the arm?" She sat up.

"Still stingin' somethin' fierce." Carsten peered out of the window.

"Marshal!" A deputy called from the sheriff's office.

Carsten squinted. The deputy raised a hand. He showed five fingers and then held up two. He pointed at the road leading into town.

"Riders." Carsten drew his Colt Frontier out of its holster and checked it. "This could be good or bad. We'd best get ready."

After getting dressed, Carsten and Fleur stepped outside. Seven riders approached on the horizon. Carsten looked across the street. Moses appeared in the window of the marshal's office with his shotgun at the ready. Wilkins stood behind him with one of his revolvers drawn. Nastas and Ramona stood on the roof of the office with their Winchesters. Few townspeople stayed on the streets.

Carsten pulled back the hammer on his Colt. "This is US Marshal Carsten McNeil!" Carsten shouted toward the riders. "State your business!"

"We're deputy marshals!" one rider called. "We received your wire."

Carsten uncocked the revolver and rotated the cylinder back to the empty chamber. He gestured for the deputies to lower their weapons.

The riders approached the sheriff's office and dismounted. Carsten nodded at the badges on their lapels.

"Is that all?" Ramona stepped forward. "Will we have enough?"

"Patterson said Boon's got at least thirty people," Carsten replied. "But we don't need lawmen. Someone get Patterson and Frazer out here. With Reid and Snow dead, I reckon Mr. Boon won't have as tight a grip on this sleepy little burg."

"What's the plan, Marshal?" one of the new deputies asked.

"We're raidin' a ranch in this area," Carsten said.

"Are these all of your men?" Hank looked them over as a deputy led him and Frazer outside.

"For the moment." Carsten looked around.

Several townspeople stepped outside to view the crowd.

"Now's the chance to find out if you're right," Fleur said.

"Do I have y'all's attention?" Carsten mounted his horse. "I'm Carsten McNeil, US Marshal for the Arizona Territory. I'm here to bring the land baron and criminal Milt Boon to justice. He's shelterin' outlaws and kidnaps women to press into service. Now, I know he likely installed Willie Snow as the sheriff here to keep a tab on what goes on 'round here. I also know his foreman, Norman Reid, was a gunfighter with a reputation. Y'all were afraid of them both, and I understand that. But neither of them are gonna be a problem anymore. If you're tired of Milt Boon, then ride with us, and together we'll bring him down. Who's with me?"

The crowd stayed silent. Some people wandered away.

"I'll ride with you," Frazer said. "I want my land back. I'm sure I have some hands willin' to join me."

"Me too!" Hank added. "That weasel cheated me outta some promised cattle, and I wanna repay the favor."

"When do we ride out?" Ramona asked.

"It's Friday today," Carsten said. "So we'll head out tomorrow. Anyone who's with me should meet us out here tomorrow afternoon. We'll ride out at dusk."

Chapter 19
Showdown at
Boon Ranch

The following day, Carsten leaned on the hitching post outside the sheriff's office. The late afternoon sun cast shadows across the streets and bathed him in shade. He nursed his bandaged arm. Fleur stood beside him. His deputies gathered. Frazer appeared with five of his ranch hands. Hank and six of his ranch hands joined them. Some only carried revolvers. Others had shotguns or repeaters. They exchanged glares.

"I know what y'all are thinkin'." Carsten stepped forward. "You've been exchangin' lead for some time, thanks to this little feud of yours. But it's time to put that bad blood behind you. There's a fella out there whose arrest is in everyone's interest. If y'all want to ride with me, you gotta agree to work together. Anybody who's got issues workin' with Patterson or Frazer boys is free to leave right now."

The ranch hands nodded in agreement. Patterson and Frazer approached each other and shook hands. Carsten gave them a proud smile.

"How many men have we got?" Fleur asked.

"I count ten sworn-in deputies," Carsten replied. "Plus a dozen ranchers, Ramona, and the six of us. It's now or never. Mount up!"

The sun set as Carsten's posse rode out toward the Boon spread.

About three-quarters of the way to the compound, Carsten gestured for them to halt near an old tree. "Dismount and gather 'round." He clambered out of his saddle.

"What's our plan of attack?" Wilkins asked.

Carsten snapped a large stick from the tree and began drawing in the dirt while the posse members thronged around the lines he made. "I got to scout out the compound thanks to a search warrant," he said. "It's gonna be the heel-toe express from here. It's Saturday night, so I reckon most of the men will be pretty roostered. Boon might have a couple of guards on watch, most likely near the gates. I'll need a couple of sure-footed volunteers to make sure they don't alert nobody."

Nastas raised a hand.

Carsten nodded. "Once the sentries by the gate are dealt with, we can sneak inside. If we can surround them, that might convince them to surrender without a fight. Boon's got several workin' girls he's kidnapped, so I must press to keep the shootin' to a minimum until we can get them to safety. Everybody got that?"

The posse nodded in agreement.

"Good," he said. "From this point on, we make no more noise than we have to. No talkin', tread quietly, and everyone stay together."

***

Night had fallen by the time the compound came into view. Carsten took several deep breaths as the posse walked down the trail. He checked his Colt Frontier and his Remington. Boisterous singing and guitar music emanated from behind the walls. A small lantern glow appeared by the gates. Carsten squinted to see a lone guard on a stool outside the small shack with the lantern resting by his feet.

Carsten lay on the ground, gesturing for the others to do the same. He patted Nastas on the shoulder. "Looks like he's loafin'," he whispered to the scout. "Good luck."

Nastas got to his feet but kept low. He shuffled toward the gates until disappearing from Carsten's view behind the guard shack. The guard picked up his rifle and lantern and stood up. Carsten held his breath.

The guard surveyed the gate. Nothing. He stepped out toward the trail. Nastas emerged from behind the shack and thumped the guard in the head with the butt of his rifle. The man fell limp, unconscious. The scout grabbed the lantern and set it down. He dragged the guard into the shack then emerged and waved toward the posse.

"Let's go," Carsten mouthed. He stood up and gestured for the deputies to follow and made his way toward the gates.

Nastas clambered onto the roof of the shack then jumped across the wall. The posse reached the gates. Carsten drew his Colt Frontier. The gates opened. Nastas peered out and gestured for them to enter.

The music and singing grew louder once inside the compound. The smell of wood smoke became prevalent.

Three large fire pits illuminated the yard, surrounded by long tables. Boon's men sat and feasted, drinking whiskey from the bottle while singing or laughing.

Carsten gestured for his posse to fan out. He surveyed the yard. The four Mexican women sat huddled at one end of the table. He counted to twenty in his head.

"Everyone's in position," Fleur said.

"US Marshals!" Carsten fired two shots into the air.

The music and laughter died down. Wilkins cocked one of his revolvers. The other deputies followed. Guns cocked across the yard, the echo carrying across the night.

"You're surrounded," Carsten said. "So you'd best stay put. Throw up your hands. You're all under arrest."

The men on the tables stayed seated. A few murmured to each other.

"Someone get those women out of here," Carsten ordered.

Fleur nodded and moved toward them.

Two of the outlaws exchanged a nod. They stood and drew their guns.

"Look out!" Wilkins fired a shot at one of them.

Carsten fired at the other. "Hold it!" he yelled. "We ain't gonna kill nobody else if y'all stay put!"

More shots rang out. Carsten saw muzzle flashes from the windows of the house. Others came from the barn, the bunkhouse, and the cantina. Two deputies fell to the ground.

"Take cover!" He fired at a rifleman in the loft.

The attacker fell from his vantage point with a short scream. Carsten fired more shots and dived behind the shed. He saw the men at the tables draw guns and return fire. The outlaws flipped the tables. A hail of gunfire tore through the shed. Splinters flew. Fleur and Wilkins took cover beside him. Wilkins fired two more shots. He tossed the empty gun aside and drew his second one.

"What's the plan?" Fleur yelled.

"We need to get those women out of the compound!" Carsten reloaded his Colt and glimpsed the four women cowering behind one table. "Keep me covered."

"Now!" Wilkins fired at Boon's men.

Carsten ran out from behind the shed. He glimpsed Todd Moony hiding behind the overturned table with the working girls. Carsten fired, and the bullet struck Todd's chest. He stumbled onto the table.

"Come on!" Carsten gestured for the women to follow him.

Ramona emerged from behind a chuck wagon. She fired her repeater from the hip. She made her way to Carsten's position. "¡Vamos!" she yelled. "¡Rapido!"

Bullets flew past as Carsten and Ramona led the women to the compound gates. Wilkins and Fleur ran close behind to bring up the rear.

"Is that everyone?" Carsten shouted above the continued gunfire.

Ramona translated his question. One woman jabbered a frightened response, too quick for Carsten to understand.

"She says there's a red-haired gringa in the hacienda," Ramona said.

"We got too many rips in the bunkhouse!" Moses retreated toward the gate. "But I got a plan. I picked this up from Reid."

He produced the bundle of dynamite.

"Blow the bunkhouse." Carsten nodded. "It might flush them out."

Moses lit the dynamite and lumbered back through the gates.

"Cover him!" Carsten peered through the gateway and returned fire.

The sound of gunfire died down near the bunkhouse and several men dashed out of the doors. A moment later, an explosion obliterated the building. Splinters and debris scattered across the compound.

Carsten ran in. Several outlaws emerged from the cantina with their hands raised. The smell of smoke filled his nostrils. He ran to the house and barged through the doors. Carsten grunted as he tumbled into the foyer. He tumbled over his wounded arm. He looked around. Several men lay dead near the windows. Others fled down the staircase. They ignored him as he made his way to the back door.

"McNeil!" a commanding voice echoed from the upper floor.

Carsten aimed his gun toward the stairs.

Milt descended the staircase a step at a time. He held an arm around Amy Filmore's neck and aimed a revolver at her head. "Drop the gun, or she dies."

Carsten tossed the Colt aside. He shut out Amy's whimpering. "Give yourself up, Boon. Most of your men are dead, surrendered, or have lit out. You can either die here or hang at Judge Stanley's convenience."

"Those aren't options, Marshal," Boon said. "I'm leaving. And I'm taking Miss Filmore with me."

"You know I'll still go after you," Carsten replied. "She already got word back to her brother. And he got word to the US Marshals. You can't run forever."

Amy's whimpering stopped at the mention of her brother.

"I will not count," Boon snarled. "Either you let me through, or I'll kill her."

Amy stomped on his toe.

Boon yelled in pain, and she wrenched free of his grasp. "You bawd!" He raised his revolver.

Carsten drew his Remington and fired. Boon fell silent as he rolled down the stairs. Carsten walked over to the body. A bullet hole went through Boon's forehead. Amy clung to the bannister and trembled.

"Are you okay, Miss Filmore?" Carsten walked up and extended his hand.

She nodded, and he led her downstairs.

Outside, the gunfire had died down. Bodies lay strewn across the compound, both Carsten's posse and Boon's men. Ten outlaws knelt by the firepits with their hands over their heads. Deputies disarmed and handcuffed them.

"Carsten!" Fleur ran over and embraced him. "You're alive!"

"What about Mr. Boon?" Hank stepped forward.

"Dead," Carsten replied. "What's the situation?"

"Most of the men lit out when the bunkhouse blew." Wilkins twirled an empty revolver. "We rounded up this bunch, but the rest escaped."

"We'll find them soon enough." Carsten turned to his wife. "But for now, let's go home."

Epilogue
Three Months Later

Carsten wiped sweat from his brow as he surveyed the herd grazing on the family's pasture.

His brother Morris rode beside him. "Nothin' like drivin' the herd. Did you miss it?"

"I reckon," Carsten replied. "A lot easier now that my arm's healed."

The two ranch hands, Davey Townsend and Mike Parrish, rode beside them.

"Do you miss bein' a lawman?" Davey asked with a grin.

"Sometimes," Carsten replied. "But things are kinda quiet in these parts. And Fleur's happier here. I reckon things got lonely in Phoenix for the both of us. I'm kinda glad to be back. How're things at home?"

"Attie's doin' fine with the baby." Davey smiled. "I'm hopin' little Jonah will grow up real strong like his uncles. How's the new house? Comfortable?"

"It suits me and Fleur," Carsten said. "And there's plenty of room."

"What for?" Morris raised an eyebrow.

"I'll tell y'all at dinner tonight." Carsten tapped his nose. "You found anybody to settle down with yet?"

"Not yet," Morris said. "But there's a cattle buyer in Prescott who's lookin' for somebody to marry his daughter. I figured I might try to introduce myself."

"Well, as long as you end up marryin' for love," Carsten said. "I don't know 'bout the rest of y'all, but I'm hungry as all get out and ready to ride back."

***

They returned to the yard at sunset. They had built two more homes near the main ranch house, and a long table sat in the yard between them. Carsten's father, Vince, hobbled out of the main house with his crutch. His mother, Cassie, set the table with Fleur while his sister, Attie, cradled her child. Carsten helped his father into his seat at the head of the table.

"I must admit," Vince said, "I never thought I'd be surpassed as a lawman by one of my own sons."

"Thanks, Pa." Carsten nodded.

"What happened with that business with Mr. Boon?" Vince gestured for Carsten to sit beside him. "It sounds like he was up to some shadier business than the others you've dealt with."

"He certainly felt like Moraday and Garrett rolled into one," Carsten said. "You always put it best: power's like drink. And he couldn't handle it. Ramona went across the border with the four Mexican women he kidnapped. She's been tryin' to reunite them with their families. As for Miss Filmore, she's gone back to Boston to live with her brother."

"I hope she can cope." Cassie brought a large stewpot to the table. "Her ordeal sounds rough. What about those feuding families?"

"They're rebuildin'," Carsten replied. "Now Mr. Boon's outta the picture. That land is up for grabs. Judge Stanley ruled Boon's herd should be sold off, and the proceeds went to both families."

"That's wonderful." Cassie doled a ladle of stew into a bowl and passed it to him.

"Who's replaced you?" Morris sat down and took his own bowl.

"Wilkins filled the top spot." Carsten smiled as Fleur emerged with a basket of cornbread. "Sure, he's only got one arm, but he's one of the best lawmen I ever worked with. That Clifford fella went back to workin' in the courts, but I hear he's good at unearthin' stuff that gets recorded there. Brennan and Nastas still serve under Wilkins."

The rest of the family joined them at the table. Morris sat in the seat beside Carsten, followed by Davey and Mike. Cassie, Fleur, and Attie sat on the opposite side of the table. Carsten breathed in the stew's smell. He bowed his head and clasped his hands.

"Come, Lord Jesus, be our guest," Vince said, "and bless what you have bestowed. Amen."

"Amen," the rest of the family said in unison.

Carsten took some cornbread and broke it up in the stew.

Fleur smiled at him. "Do you want to say, or shall I?"

The rest of the family fell silent and looked toward them.

"Has somethin' happened?" Morris asked.

"Matter of fact, it has." Carsten beamed. "Why don't you tell 'em, darlin'?"

"I'm expectin'," Fleur said with a smile.

The other family members clapped and cheered. Vince gave Carsten a proud smile.

"That's great!" Attie said. "You got any ideas for names?"

"Been thinkin' on that a spell." Carsten rubbed his chin. "If it's a boy, I reckon we're gonna call him Ezra." He looked toward the grave markers overlooking the ranch.

"And if it's a girl," Fleur added, "I suggested Blanche. That was my mother's name."

"You'll make a noble father, son," Vince said. "I know you will."

The End

Thanks for taking the time to read this story. A positive review on Amazon would be appreciated.